SLEEPER TRAIN

JAY BOWER
JOHN LYNCH

SHADOW FOREST
PUBLISHING

PROLOGUE

The rain poured down on the arched glass ceiling high above the train platform. The Coastal Express was preparing for its maiden voyage, crossing the United States from New York City to San Francisco. The proprietors of the new venture, Boulder and Smith, had advertised it as luxury on rails. Their promotional material talked about how it was like the Titanic, without icebergs, of course. Only the richest and most powerful people could hope to attain a seat on the opulent masterpiece.

It was the perfect opportunity for Matthew Gladstone to prove to his girlfriend, Amanda Mitchell, that he was swimming in cash. Between the trust fund his parents bestowed on him and the massive gains he made with insider tips on the stock market, he could burn his cash and still have more money than 90% of other people his age. Being rich at twenty-seven was an asset he shoved in everyone's face and for some reason Amanda still doubted the extent of his wealth. He was determined to prove it to her, and booking the trip aboard the Coastal Express was the perfect opportunity.

"They don't let just anyone on this train," Matthew said, "only those that are worthy." Amanda's plump lips turned up in a smile. She looked at the other waiting passengers. Matthew followed her gaze toward a couple not too far from them. The older man wore a pressed Armani suit that was a dark shade of gray, which contrasted with his neatly trimmed white goatee. His tanned, bald head shone in the lights of the station. The woman was considerably younger, blonde, and curvy.

"That's got to be his mistress," Matthew whispered. "She's way too young for him."

"Not unless it's his daughter."

"Highly unlikely. You do remember the pitch for this train, right?"

What intrigued Matthew more than the uber-rich exclusivity was the hedonistic nature of the trip. Not only were passengers afforded a cross-country trip in the nicest train ever built, but they were also given free rein to indulge in every sexual fantasy they could imagine, and he had plenty he wanted to try with Amanda.

"I suppose that would be weird," Amanda said, "but they did say anything goes."

"True." Now curious, Matthew watched the pair, trying to determine if they were here together, or *together.*

A loud train whistle reverberated throughout the station, and Matthew's excitement skyrocketed. He fidgeted his fingers, slowly running them along the hem of his light wool coat.

An old-style steam-powered locomotive pulled into the station. The engine was black with red accents. It pulled a number of sleeper cars, a dining car, two other cars that Matthew wasn't aware of their purpose, and a traditional caboose. From the outside, it appeared like any other train, something Boulder and Smith, the proprietors, took painstaking measures to ensure. They wanted the train to appear normal from the outside, a stark contrast to the happenings *inside*.

"Are you ready?" Matthew asked Amanda.

She slipped her hand in his and squeezed. "I'm getting wet just thinking about it."

She wasn't a prude, but Amanda hadn't often spoken so openly before. Matthew had a good feeling about this. He adjusted himself, hiding his erection.

The train came to a stop. Its doors opened and the awaiting passengers filtered inside.

"Wow," Amanda said when they stepped inside. Matthew felt the same way. Dark mahogany panels, gold accents, plush velvet cushions in a deep shade of crimson. The floor was carpeted in a similar color of red. A scent of vanilla with a hint of lilac permeated the air.

"Mr. Ivory?" a man asked. A physique like a pro wrestler, he was dressed in black pants and a black vest over a white dress shirt. He wore thin white gloves. Matthew looked at the other employees and they all wore the same gloves.

"Mr. Ivory?" the man asked again. It took a moment before Matthew remembered the false moniker he'd registered under, a requirement for all passengers.

"Yes?" Matthew replied.

"Your ticket, please?" Matthew handed him both his and Amanda's tickets.

"This way, sir," the man said. Matthew assumed he was some sort of butler, as were the others. He and Amanda followed him to a room with a '*32*' marked outside the door in shiny gold numbers.

"Your room, sir. Once you enter, all your desires are free to explore. Welcome aboard the Coastal Express. Enjoy your stay." He handed Matthew a key. "For your room, sir. Only you can open it. No other passenger has access to your room, unless, of course, you allow it. We hold master keys, but they are used only in case of emergencies. Once you lock the door from the inside, no one is getting in unless you invite them."

Matthew and Amanda stepped inside, and the butler closed the door behind them. The loud click of the latch seemed to emphasize the man's insistence on the room's security.

"It's much bigger than I thought it would be," Amanda said. "From the outside it doesn't look like much, but…wow."

Matthew felt the same way, marveling at the exquisite detail of the room.

"Hey, look," Matthew said. A bottle of bourbon sat on a small wooden table near the window with two small glasses next to it. Both glasses were filled with ice.

"They must have just filled these before the train came in. The ice hasn't even melted!" Amanda said.

"Now *this* is living," Matthew said. He opened the bottle and poured drinks for them both, handing one to Amanda. "To a trip we won't forget," he said, raising his glass in a toast.

Matthew locked the door, and they took their seats, looking out the window which faced opposite the train plat-form. Inside, the train station was filled with travel posters depicting some of the sights they'd see along the way: the Appalachian Mountains, the St. Louis Arch, Texas Prairies, the Rocky Mountains, deserts, and more. Matthew hoped he'd be too busy with Amanda to do much sightseeing.

Moments later, the train moved.

"Off we go," Matthew said. As if he spoke it into existence, the train lurched forward, and the station swiftly moved past.

"You know the individual rooms are soundproof, don't you?" Matthew asked.

"No, I didn't."

"That means we can get as loud as we want in here and no one will know. Kinda liberating, isn't it?"

Amanda sipped her drink and smiled. "Yes, yes, it is."

Before they left the city, the pair had begun kissing and Matthew's excitement grew along with his erection, which was back in full force.

When the train entered the New York countryside, he ripped off Amanda's shirt and tossed it aside. Her large breasts shook with the movement of the train. She unhooked her bra and exposed her bare chest, her dark nipples hardening.

"Fuck, yes," Matthew said. He pulled off his shirt. Toned from hours spent in the gym, he relished any chance to take his shirt off in front of the opposite sex. He crouched in front of her and slipped off her pants. She wasn't wearing any panties underneath. He smiled and looked up at her.

"I was prepared," she said, sporting a devilish grin.

Matthew leaned forward and spread her legs. He licked his lips, taking in the view of her well-groomed vagina. Her scent drew him in, and he flicked her skin with his tongue. He knew she was ready, but he really wanted to rev her engine, so he lightly ran his fingers across her vulva, taking care to not hastily go straight for the clit. He massaged her inner thighs and lower belly, kissing and tickling. Always going toward her clitoris, but not touching it. Yet. He continued stroking and massaging her, allowing her to relax and get used to his touch. Amanda moaned, writhing about.

Matthew knew it was almost time, but he wanted to tease her a little more. He started using acupressure, running his finger along her vagina, up to the clit but still not touching it yet. She glistened, moaning louder, and now Matthew dove in. He spread her open, exposing her fully engorged clit. Using his tongue, he made circular motions on her clit, periodically stopping to flick at it so she wouldn't grow numb to the circular motions. He kept at it for a while. Once he'd gotten into a rhythm that worked for her, it became easier. Before long, her vocalizations grew louder, her breaths coming at quicker intervals. He gently sucked her clit, something he knew she loved.

Amanda grasped his head and shoved his face further into her. Matthew was surrounded by her sweet aroma and his cock felt like it was going to explode.

"That's it, baby," she said. "Just like that. Unnhhh, don't stop."

Like a gentleman, Matthew obliged his woman, eager to make her cum in his mouth.

Someone knocked on the door and Amanda squealed.

Matthew pulled back. "What the fuck?" he said breathlessly.

The knock sounded again, this time more forcefully.

"Go away," Matthew said. "This room is taken."

The knocking grew more persistent.

"Just…answer it. I can't concentrate with them pounding like that. I'll be here waiting," Amanda said, slipping her fingers inside her wet pussy. She pulled them out and ran her fingers across his lips before covering herself.

Matthew groaned but got up and answered the door.

"Who is it?" he grumbled.

It was the older, bald man from the platform. The one who Matthew thought had brought his daughter.

"Am I interrupting?" the man asked. For a moment, Matthew thought he was looking at an older, bearded Lex Luthor in a designer suit, but dismissed the idea.

"Yeah, you are. What do you want?"

The man tsk'd. "Is that some way to talk to your neighbor?"

"Look, man. We're kinda in the middle of something here."

The train rocked back and forth, both men reached for the door frame. The bald man, steadying himself. Matthew, blocking the entrance.

"I won't be long."

"What?" Matthew asked, confused by the statement.

The man lunged into Matthew, knocking him across the room and against the window. With Matthew out of the way, he spun around, locked the door, and then turned back to the couple before Matthew had a chance to recover.

"I've been waiting for this," the man said. He extracted a large meat cleaver from inside his jacket. He smiled and swung the blade in a downward arc, lodging it in Matthew's skull. Blood splashed from the wound.

Amanda let out a blood-curdling scream. Matthew groaned, the expression on his face a mixture of pain and shock.

The man pulled the cleaver free, and as Matthew slumped

over, the man chopped the blade sideways, hacking into Matthew's neck, another splash of blood painting both the window and Amanda's bare chest.

Amanda thrust herself away from the assailant, but he grabbed her by the hair and slammed her against the wall. The impact knocked the wind out of her.

"Not yet," he snarled.

Somehow, against all odds, Matthew clung to life, weakly swatting at the man, but his efforts were for nothing. He was as good as dead.

Amanda screamed and thrashed. The man pulled the cleaver free of its home in Matthew's neck. With the blade free, blood squirted from the severed artery, hastily ushering Matthew out of the land of the living.

The man swung the weapon at Amanda and caught her just above the collarbone. The blade dragged across her flesh, leaving a deep wound. She threw a punch, hitting him on the arm, and he smacked her. The blow was so hard it dislodged a tooth and sent it arcing across the room.

Furious, the man swung the cleaver repeatedly, blood spraying into the air and puddling into the velvety carpet. The window was painted with gore. Amanda cried out, but the man continued to hack into her flesh.

Amanda was long dead before the man finally ceased his assault. He wiped the blade on the curtain before slipping it back inside his coat, which was now sopping with blood and flecks of flesh and tissue. He gave himself a once over in the mirror and realized he'd need to cover the evidence a bit before leaving the room. Cleanup of the bodies would be taken care of, but it wouldn't suit his purposes to alert anyone to what he was up to this early on the voyage.

The man entered the bathroom and cleaned up as best he could. The jacket and undershirt were both ruined, so he removed both and placed them in the trash. Wearing a plain white t-shirt and dress pants, the man wrapped the blade in a towel and exited the room.

CHAPTER 1

Kurt and Emily Meyer held each other's hands as they stood on the train platform. Kurt felt the sweat roll down his back despite the cold air swirling around them. He'd saved for months to secure their tickets for the Coastal Express. When he surprised Emily with them for their anniversary, she had reacted with disinterest, claiming the motion of trains made her stomach churn and they'd be better off going on a trip to Gatlinburg. Kurt dismissed her reservations and convinced her that they'd be fine on the train. Besides, he argued, he'd heard all limits were off once they were on the train, and *that* seemed to promise an atmosphere that would lead to rekindling Emily's inner naughty side.

Early in their marriage, Emily was often eager to try new things in the bedroom. There were months when she'd beg him to fuck her in the ass or spank her so hard her ass would have marks that wouldn't fade for days. But that was years ago. Now, he was lucky if she'd give him a blow job, and he had a better chance of seeing Jesus Christ in the flesh than a position other than missionary. Even then, it was only on certain days of the week. Their sex life had turned stale, which was part of the reason that Kurt had worked tirelessly to convince Emily of the trip's worth.

They had no children, but not for lack of desire. They tried, especially early in the marriage, but eventually after many, many failures, they'd both undergone tests only to discover Kurt was shooting blanks and Emily had uterine cysts. It was as if the universe itself had conspired against them, doing its damnedest to condemn Mr. and Mrs. Meyer to a quiet home with no legacy left behind.

Soon after the bad news, Emily brought up the idea of adoption. They'd almost gone through with it, but in the end, it fell through because Kurt had backed out at the eleventh hour. Often, he felt like she still resented him for it, but he still stood by the decision. How would it make sense to adopt a child when he didn't have his heart set on it? How would that be fair for himself, or the child? Ten years in the past, and still those ghosts haunted them. They'd buried their grief inside their jobs instead of comforting each other and the result was the loss of a vibrant connection, replaced by the shell of a marriage they found themselves in.

But all the heartache and loss of togetherness is what forced Kurt to seek something different, something exciting. He tried that once with a co-worker, a mistake he never should've made. But they were here now. Maybe their relationship wasn't dead and buried just yet.

One of his friends at Goose Heart Marketing, the ad agency where he worked, suggested he consider the Coastal Express. A trip so exclusive it wasn't explicitly marketed by the agency but was something known to insiders. At first put off by their exorbitant prices, Kurt's friend encouraged him by sharing his own experience on board and how it supercharged his relationship with his wife. That gave him the nudge he needed to make the decision. Having a cross-country trip where he and Emily could rekindle their youthful sexual fantasies meant they'd have a chance to spark an intimacy they had both let die.

And despite her reservations about the booking, Kurt knew her agreeing to the trip meant she wasn't ready to give up on what they once had, either.

The train whistle blew and jolted Kurt back to the present. The warmth of Emily's hand in his felt perfect.

"Are you ready?" he asked. She smiled up at him. He was close to a foot taller than her, and she was 5' 2" on a good day. Curly red hair framed her pale face. Faint freckles on her cheeks were like constellations that he'd always marveled at.

"I think so," she replied. "Are you?"

Kurt wasn't sure. He thought he was, but in the back of his mind, he worried what the future may hold. He had a bad habit of letting his mind spiral with negative thoughts. What if things didn't go as planned? Then what would they do? They were stuck on a 20 day round-trip excursion from New York to San Francisco and back. What if, along the way, Emily decided that unlimited sexual fantasies weren't appealing? It was entirely possible. Sure, they'd both fallen off, but in the end hot, steamy sex took two people, and Kurt was only one person. And while she was here for the same reason he was, it was entirely possible she'd change her mind. The thought of this going bad and being stuck on the train for three weeks of hell almost made him want to turn around and go home before the trip got started.

"Honey?" she asked. He noticed she had a worried look on her face. "Are you ok?"

He smiled, her soft voice correcting his spiraling mind. "Yeah, I was just lost in thought. I think we're going to have the time of our lives. It'll be like the old days." His voice didn't betray his lack of conviction.

"You say old days like we've been married fifty years! It's only been ten."

"You know what I mean. I miss us. I miss what we were," Kurt said.

The train whistle blew louder, and they could see it in the distance, heading for the station. Smoke billowed out of the stack on the engine.

"We're still that couple. The only thing that's changed is that we're older, more secure in who we are. More mature," Emily said.

Kurt groaned internally but kept his thoughts to himself. Mature. That was the word Emily used often. He understood that to mean she no longer cared about bonding with him intimately. Sex was just an afterthought, a dirty little act she consented to on occasion and not necessarily because she wanted to enjoy him. Her use of it here on the train did not bode well, unless of course he was letting the intrusive thoughts win again.

The locomotive pulling into the station stole his attention. He'd always loved trains and had wanted to get a toy version complete with a rolling countryside and a little town. Riding on one like this was fulfilling a boyhood fantasy. If things went well with Emily, he'd be fulfilling far more fantasies, and once more the mental seesaw he'd been on regarding his sexual prospects aboard the train went in the opposite direction.

Emily let go of his hand and lifted the handle on her suitcase. They were told to bring the essentials and only a few changes of clothes. Onboard laundry services would take care of what they needed, plus each room came with several changes of loungewear, the idea being that passengers would rarely leave their rooms.

The train stopped and let out a whoosh of steam. The platform buzzed with the conversation of the awaiting passengers and the atmosphere felt electric with the collective excitement of those waiting to board, Kurt and Emily included.

The boarding doors opened, and thickly muscled men stepped out. They were all adorned like butlers with thin white gloves and black vests over white dress shirts.

"This way," one of them called out, waving the passengers toward the train. Kurt noticed there were several faces in the windows inside the train peering out at them. He figured they must have boarded at one of the earlier stations.

Kurt and Emily got in line. "Remember, we're the Heart's, not the Meyer's," Kurt whispered. Emily nodded. They were all given assumed names for the trip, a layer of protection for passengers. Boulder and Smith found themselves up to their ears in pending litigation over the "depraved" train's maiden trip, and many former passengers found themselves involved as well. And then, like magic, a windfall of settlements materialized, and litigation was dropped. Shortly after, false identities for "protection" became a requirement to book the trip.

The line moved quickly as the muscled butlers hurried the onboarding passengers into the bowels of the train. When

Kurt and Emily were next in line, one of the men fake smiled and put his hand out. "Tickets?" the man grunted.

Kurt handed them over.

"Ah, yes. Mr. And Mrs. Heart. This way, please." His pleasant demeanor and softly spoken words were a harsh contrast to his gruff call for their tickets. He turned and headed into the train with Kurt and Emily trying to keep up.

The butler walked them through the train, explaining details that went in one ear and out the other as they moved until they reached room 23.

"And here we are," the man said. He held out a key and pressed it into Kurt's hand. "Protect this key. Each reservation comes with one. If you misplace it, we can unlock your room with the master key, but that is an extra you will be charged for. We don't make extra keys on board, and each use of the master key is a charge."

"Jeez," Emily said, "Really trying to nickel and dime everyone even after the money we spent?"

The man smiled but said nothing.

"Just open the door, please," Kurt said.

"We place a high priority on the privacy of our guests. No one is allowed in your room without your express permission. As you know, our guests are free to fulfill all their desires and sometimes other guests can be... a bit crafty about joining the fun. We control room access by giving only the occupants their single key. We find that this process encourages our guests to take special care with their key. We trust you to hold on to it. Breaking that trust comes with consequences."

"Understood," Kurt said, rolling his eyes so hard his retinas threatened to detach. "We'll protect it with our lives."

If the man was put off by the snark in Kurt's voice, he gave no indication, simply responded with a slight nod of his head before ending with, "If you need anything, there's a phone to call for refreshments such as drink or food. If you require any additional items to enhance your pleasure, you may call for those as well."

Kurt noticed Emily's cheeks redden. He wondered what they offered, and if Emily would be up for trying whatever it was they had. If the items were brand new, he hoped she'd be game.

The man turned and closed the door behind him, the latch locking as he did.

"Ready?" Kurt asked. He shifted their luggage to a shelf on the far-left side of their quarters.

Emily sat on the long, velvety bench and propped her legs up. For a moment *Greek goddess* was the term that popped into Kurt's head. Emily was that striking.

"Yes, I think I am." She smiled and Kurt felt a tingle in his pants. Maybe this trip was going to be better than he imagined.

<h1 style="text-align:center">CHAPTER 2</h1>

Robert Colton had seen a lot of crazy shit in his time as a U.S. Marshal. Ten years on the job wasn't much in comparison to many of the other Marshals he served with, but it was enough time to experience things most men never did. Judicial security, prisoner transportation, fugitive task forces, witness security. You name it, Robert had done it.

But an undercover investigation of the notorious serial killer, *The Rail Car Cleaver*, might just be the thing that stamps his career. Robert didn't want to simply be a Marshal, he wanted to be *the* Marshal. A man with a status so legendary, his name was revered amongst his peers. Whispered about by his fellow Marshals. Admired. It was why he had become a Marshal to begin with. Bullied as a child, Robert had promised himself when he was older, he would bring the real bullies, the *bad guys,* to justice.

Of course, as time and experience desensitized him, he himself had become a bully. Never of the innocent, but to those who were the worst of the worst, Robert was a nightmare. It wasn't something that came naturally to him, and he'd worked hard to develop a spine. Now, he might as well be made of fucking ice.

Robert milled about with the boarding passengers of The Coastal Express, doing his best to fit in. Fitting in with this crowd was another thing that was not natural for him. All the passengers were filthy rich, something Robert knew nothing about. He'd spent countless hours over the last few months, long days and sleepless nights adopting a new persona. It was tough, but Robert was the best the Marshals had at under-cover operations. If he couldn't do it, it was impossible.

But the more he thought about the task at hand, he wasn't sure he was the man for the job. For the first time in his career, Robert wasn't sure if the mission could be completed.

They'd received an anonymous tip about the Rail Car Cleaver a few months ago. Word had it he'd grown tired of chopping up bums and whores along America's railways and was ready to move on to something that would cement him as America's most infamous serial killer. What better way to make your mark than a killing spree of the elite? People so cash rich they could afford a luxury, hedonistic train ride. A train ride so secretive, the passengers all assumed pseudonyms if the manifest was anything to go by. For whatever reason, the men and women boarding this train with him wanted no ties to the trip, and they all had enough money to make it happen.

Shuffling among the other passengers, Colton thought long and hard about the anonymous tip. The more he thought about it, the more positive he became that the call had come from none other than the Rail Car Cleaver himself. It wasn't unheard of. If the call had indeed come from the man himself, it would hardly be the first time a serial killer attempted to toy with law enforcement while striking fear into the hearts of law-abiding citizens.

There wasn't much of a profile on the killer, for as advanced as things were in 1996, building a profile was still difficult work, and the killer hadn't left much to go by. Even Colton's guess the call had come from the Cleaver was nothing more than a gut feeling. In truth, the shared information between all agencies on the Cleaver amounted to squat, and if not for the call inviting them to this game of cat and mouse, it was more than likely they'd all still be in the dark and the Rail Car Cleaver would be free to dismember at will.

And there was something else, something that left a sour feeling in the pit of his stomach. Adopting a false, rich persona was only one point of trouble for the mission. And if having minimal information on the Rail Car Cleaver wasn't bad enough, Colton and the information specialists at his disposal had been able to gather fuck all when it came to information about both The Coastal Express, and its proprietors, Boulder and Smith. It wasn't for lack of trying. They had the best of the best under their employ, and available for contract work, yet they remained empty-handed. All they'd managed to discover was the decadent, secretive nature of The Coastal Express. Somehow, information on the proprietors was similarly impossible to come by, nothing more than brief biographical information and fluff pieces about business ventures.

So where did the money come from? And why have the feds never investigated the two when the math clearly didn't add up? During the investigation, something else that was odd popped up. Strange at first, almost as if it were a mistake. But a word kept surfacing. No context, no further information, or anything it might tie to: *Sleepers.* What the fuck was a sleeper?

Something about it made Colton's skin crawl and gave him heartburn. But Colton was nothing if not a professional. If the Rail Car Cleaver were aboard The Coastal Express, he'd find him and bring him to justice. And if he had any say in the matter, he'd pierce through the veil of secrecy shrouding Boulder and Smith and shine a light on them and whatever the hell the *sleepers* were.

A gentleman dressed in black and white broke his trance. "Sir?" the man asked.

"What is it?"

"I said I would escort you to your room if you would kindly show me your ticket, sir."

Colton let out a long sigh, playing the part of bothered wealth. "As if I need assistance from the likes of you," he replied.

If the man was bothered by Colton's dig, he gave no indication. Colton figured, given his occupation, he had likely gotten used to being spoken down to. He almost felt bad for the man, but something was off. He was different than the typical hired help. His physical stature, for one. Underneath the vest and the dress attire, Colton could see was the body of a man built more like Carl Weathers than a glorified butler. It was possible the service staff doubled as security, or whatever passed for security on board The Coastal Express, but again, his instincts told him that wasn't the case.

Something to keep an eye on, at least. In his training, Colton had become a master at situational awareness, noticing those present, identifying possible threats and avenues of escape. While digging in his breast pocket for the ticket, he noticed that Apollo Creed wasn't the only member of the train's service staff with the physique of an 80s action hero, in fact, every member of the staff he'd seen so far appeared to be built like a brick shithouse.

The man plucked the ticket from Colton's hand before handing it back to him. "This way, sir," he said, as he led Colton to his quarters.

Colton took care to observe his surroundings, committing anyone who looked out of place to memory. There were many people boarding the train with him, and many more had already boarded at the first of two boarding locations. This was to be the last onboarding of the entire trip. From here, there would be no stops aside from refuel checkpoints.

Colton would have liked to have boarded at the first stop, but logistics hadn't afforded him the luxury. It would have provided a better opportunity to scope out the entire train with far less people on board, and an opportunity to start profiling potential suspects far sooner, including those who'd been among the very first passengers aboard the train. What if The Cleaver had already boarded? It would certainly make the search for him more difficult. He could be anyone, anywhere.

The train was loud, the hustle and bustle of the passengers made focusing a taller task. Taller, but not insurmountable. After a lengthy walk zig zagging between couples and throuples - some of the men and women dressed as people of status, while others dressed like they were here for days of sweaty, lust driven sex - they arrived at Colton's assigned room. The man opened the door and handed him a key, explaining the details of the room. Colton let the information go in one ear and out the other, although he did make note of the man's mention of the soundproofing of the rooms. Surely an amenity meant to allow for both relaxation and privacy, but a room where sound couldn't escape would also make for a great place to dismember a human body.

Colton thanked the man and entered the cabin. He sat down and kicked his dress shoes off. The Marshals in charge of his wardrobe clearly paid no mind to comfort when selecting his wardrobe. He'd have a word with the bastards when the mission was over. He flexed his toes, stretching his feet. As he sat in the relaxing quarters, he pulled two items from the pocket inside the breast of his jacket–a small photograph and a flask with his name engraved in intricate lettering. It was against standard operating procedures to take such personal effects on undercover operations, but Colton took his baby girl with him everywhere. And lately, the flask, too. He unscrewed the cap, took a long swig of Jack Daniel's, and tossed the empty metal container aside. It was a miracle he'd maintained a high level of operation for as long as he had, with his drinking getting worse. But cracks were beginning to show, and Colton wondered how long he could keep it up for.

His throat burned and tears welled up. Colton closed his eyes and kissed the photo of his daughter, Jessica. Taken from him by a monster all those years ago.

There were monsters everywhere, and Colton would not rest until the latest monster of the week was behind bars.

CHAPTER 3

Arianna Prescott stowed her bags in the storage area of her quarters. The rooms were quite nice, and were more spacious than she'd have guessed, considering it was a train. She'd finally amassed enough money to feel comfortable in life. Of course, comfort to her meant she never had to worry about money period, and that had taken some time, patience, trips to the plastic surgeon, and the untimely deaths of a few elderly gentlemen who liked to dip their wicks in the young stuff.

The first time it happened, it hadn't been *her* choice. Her deadbeat father made the choice for her, essentially selling her to cover his gambling debts. Sixteen was the legal age of consent, and in the state of Rhode Island, so long as a legal guardian signed off, law permitted a marriage between the minor and an adult. Arianna hadn't protested. She'd simply listened to her father, who'd convinced her that not only was she going to do what was right for the family - saving her father's bacon - but she was setting herself up for an easy future. Her husband-to-be was so old it was likely she'd be widowed by twenty-five years old and the sole beneficiary of a mountain of cash and investments.

Well, he might have been a piece of shit for what he'd done, but Dad had been right about becoming a widow with money. Of course, Arianna made damn sure to hurry the process along, doing anything and everything she could to aid the decline of her paper-husband's already rapidly declining health. Not only had he bit the dust, but he'd actually kicked the bucket before her twenty-first birthday. Even still, four years of lying underneath the disgusting geezer while he pumped away at her, filling her up with his sour, geriatric cum that had the consistency of globs of gelatin was far more than she should have had to endure. She was angry at herself for allowing her father to convince her it was her duty to help him for no other reason than because they were family. But even more so, she was angry at her father for being a piece of shit dead-beat. It was a father's job to protect his daughter. To raise her properly and guide her toward the realization of her self-worth. To show her she never need settle for anything less than she deserved.

Instead, he did the opposite. He preyed on her youth, on her naivety, and on her own love of family. Rather than instill values in her, he helped to instill hatred and anger. She used those feelings, along with some of the money she'd obtained from her first inheritance, to make sure the first man to betray her, her father, found an early grave himself. Lucky for her, she had enough cash to make it happen the right way - a professional hit man. Zero chance that was going to come back and bite her in the ass. You get what you pay for.

But the money went quickly. When you're young and

sitting on tons of cash, and you've got nobody to teach you how to invest, pissing it away is as simple as snapping your fingers.

Which was why she found herself in another marriage with an elderly slimeball willing to put his fortune on the line for a warm, young body. Elderly men didn't seem to care about prior marriages. They simply wanted a trophy wife with a warm hole to fuck, for as long as his withered cock could maintain an erection. The key was finding someone likely to die on their own. She'd gotten away with ushering her first husband into a grave. No need to tempt fate and develop a pattern. Each time she got her hands dirty could potentially land her a life sentence. And of course it took research. It was imperative to make sure the old geezer didn't have family members that would come crawling out of the woodwork, upset that their daddy, or grandfather, left them out of the will. Avoiding complications was priority.

In her second marriage, Arianna had been lucky once more. Husband number two had gone even quicker than the first. The ink had hardly dried on the damned marriage certificate. Could lady luck have finally taken a shine to her? Why not? After what her father did to her, she certainly deserved to be happy. What better way to achieve that goal than through financial security?

Which was why she found husband number three. He had been a real son of a bitch, though. Somehow, dying of cancer, his death all but a forgone conclusion, he'd beaten the odds. The doctors pinned his life expectancy at roughly twelve to eighteen months. The stubborn prick refused to give up, and fought with every fiber in his being, and dollar in his bank account. When it was clear the man wasn't going to give up the ghost any time soon, she took it upon herself to summon the reaper. A bit of wolfsbane in his sunscreen had been enough to do the trick when they'd been vacationing in the east. At his age, the authorities never suspected a thing. Whether or not that was because they didn't want to deal with an investigation of foreign travelers, or they truly didn't suspect foul play, Arianna didn't know. And she sure as hell didn't care because she'd slipped up and took care of business herself again, rather than use a professional. Her youth made her prone to rash decisions. But that was over and done with. It didn't matter anymore. What mattered was the money.

And the thrill she'd experienced taking a man's life. An unexpected bonus. She hadn't felt the thrill with her first husband, but those circumstances had been different. With three bodies under her belt, she longed to feel the rush once more. Maybe here, on the train. Vacationing solo, the train wasn't the only thing she expected to ride. The more she thought about indulging in the pleasures of the flesh, as well as the rending of it, the wetter she became. Arianna rubbed her thighs together. If the rumors about this little voyage were true, she didn't think the owners would turn her in. The things that went on behind closed doors here were not the type of thing you wanted to involve the police in. Why else would everyone board under pseudonyms?

Arianna stood up and stretched her lithe body, her augmented breasts—just enough to make her feel more confident—stretching the fabric of her tight red dress. It hugged her curves in all the right places. Before she decided how far she would take things, Arianna knew she needed to get a feel for the train. The passengers and the staff. She'd make a tour of the common areas. Mingle a bit and gather as much information as she could. And maybe she would find a stud or two to fuck. After years of sleeping with elderly men, it would be nice to fill her needs with a more desirable partner.

Arianna spritzed herself with perfume, grabbed her purse, and made her way to the bar.

CHAPTER 4

Emily clung to Kurt's neck, her hot rod red fingernails piercing his flesh. He thrust into her over and over.

"Fuck me," she breathed. "Come on baby, fuck me harder."

Kurt obliged, and she moaned as he pounded her. She couldn't say why or how, but after boarding the Coastal Express, she felt her inhibitions melt away, her desire rekindled. It was like vacation sex on steroids, and she wanted more of it. They'd already fucked once soon after entering their room. Now, as the countryside rushed along outside their window, speeding toward their destination, she was speeding toward another orgasm.

Emily's pale breasts swayed with each thrust, her large pink nipples at full attention. Kurt leaned down and nibbled on one of them, and the sensation of his teeth over her sensitive flesh sent shivers through her. She lifted his head and pushed hers closer, wanting to kiss. She pressed her lips against his and their tongues danced seductively with one another, all the while she felt Kurt's cock filling her.

Harder and faster, Kurt thrust into her. The sting of their

bare flesh slapping together mingled with the welcome pleasure of a good pounding.

"Take me from behind," she moaned. She pushed him out of her and turned around, bending over with her hands against the window. Kurt slid between her legs and she felt him spread open her ass cheeks as he slipped his cock into her waiting pussy. She moaned loudly, not caring if the soundproofed rooms really worked or not. She was completely overcome by lust and didn't give a damn if anyone else knew.

Kurt slammed into her, the sound of her ass smacking against him in a rhythmic beat sent electricity through her. She glanced back and watched Kurt spit on his thumb, then he slipped it between her ass cheeks. She felt a sudden pressure on her tight hole as he slowly inserted it into her. It hurt at first, but it also felt good, and she soon became accustomed to the feeling.

Emily closed her eyes and moaned. The feeling of being filled in both holes was something she hadn't experienced in years. It was equal measures pain and pleasure, and her body responded to the sensation by producing a higher volume of transudate fluid in her vagina.

Kurt continued to thrust harder and soon Emily felt a tingling sensation. "That's it baby, give it to me." Kurt obliged, his moans increasing in volume and intensity.

She welcomed the blinding ecstasy that consumed her as the orgasm made her legs shake. It was so powerful that she nearly fell flat. Colors swirled in her vision and bursts of light blinded her.

Kurt moaned louder behind her. Barely able to register what was going on through the sensuous haze of her own orgasm, Emily found the clarity to speak. "Cum on me," she said. Kurt thrust a few more times and then pulled out. She felt his warm ejaculate spurt all over her back and ass.

They both took a moment to catch their breath. Sweat trickled down Emily's face. It had been a very long time since they had done something like that. She stood and wrapped her arms around Kurt. "I love you," she said, planting a deep kiss on his soft lips.

"I love you, too," Kurt replied.

After cleaning up, they crawled into the bed lying next to each other, Kurt's arms wrapped around Emily. She welcomed the embrace and nestled deeper into his arms. There was nowhere else in the world she'd rather be. She thought if she were to die right now, she'd die a happy woman.

HOURS AFTER THEIR FURIOUS LOVEMAKING, Emily awoke with a ravenous hunger. Since boarding the train, all she and Kurt had done was spend time in their room having sex. The release of pent-up sexual tension left her drained, her body begging her to refuel.

She climbed out of bed, leaving Kurt to rest, snoring softly. She considered waking him but thought better of it.

She threw some clothes on and took in the cabin, really absorbed it all, for what felt like the first time. She marveled at the deep mahogany wood and the rich red velvet which adorned most of the cabin. It was like a mini apartment - a bed, a couch, a small chair and table. And though it was small, there was a bathroom containing a toilet, sink, and shower.

She knew the trip had to cost a lot of money. When Kurt mentioned it to her, she acted disinterested because if she were being honest, she didn't really understand what he was explaining. She did some research and found out that most passengers were social elites with money to burn. They didn't seem to fit in with the clientele. They talked about money often, and though they weren't pinching pennies together, surely, they couldn't afford something so extravagant. Kurt assured her the money wasn't an issue and that the trip would not ruin them financially. She finally agreed, though in the back of her mind she maintained reservations.

Now, standing in the middle of their cabin surrounded by luxury, she wondered again how they could afford the trip. Not that she was complaining about it. She'd always wanted to live a life of luxury, but now that she had a taste, she felt like an imposter.

On the bed, Kurt stirred. Emily looked at him and smiled. Feelings of financial inadequacy aside, this trip could be just the thing they needed to put the spark back in their lives.

"Hey sleepy head," Emily said.

Kurt turned toward her and opened his eyes. "Hey," he replied. His stomach gurgled and Emily laughed.

"Sounds like you're as hungry as I am. Why don't we find the dining car and grab something to eat?"

"Good idea, babe." Kurt sat up and rubbed his eyes with the palms of his hands. He was never one for a nap and Emily enjoyed seeing him relax for once.

"I see you've already given their complimentary clothes a try," he said, nodding toward her. Emily looked down with a grin on her face and nodded.

"I figured they left them here for us. Why not try them?"

Each room was supplied with a few pairs of clothing. Comfy linen pants and shirts, the kind you'd expect to see on a tropical beach. Though on a train crossing the country, they were as far away from the ocean as possible, so it was a bit comical to see. They were natural colored with red thread along the seams. It didn't deter Emily from trying them on and now wearing them, she loved how airy and relaxed they felt.

"You've got some too," she said, pointing at the closet. "Try them on."

"Are you gonna wear that outside of here?" he asked. Emily hadn't bothered to put on a bra or panties and didn't think anything of it.

"Are you worried someone might see me?" she asked with a grin. She pulled the shirt tight, and her nipples visibly poked against the fabric. Despite the rough look of the cloth, it was soft against her skin.

"If you aren't, I guess I'm not either."

"Good! Come on, I'm starving."

Kurt got off the bed, planted a soft kiss on her lips, and after relieving himself, slipped into the clothes issued for him. They fit him well, accentuating his toned physique and hugging his ass, something she enjoyed watching from time to time.

"How's this?" he asked, twirling for her inspection.

"Looks a little tight in the front," she said, winking as she pointed at his crotch.

Where had all this sexual energy come from? she wondered. She'd not felt this way in a very long time and now she was acting like a teenaged boy flooded with hormones. Staring at Kurt and the bulge in his pants, she was starting to grow excited again.

Her stomach grumbled and interrupted her lustful

thoughts. She knew if they were to go another round, she'd need to refuel her body.

"I think it's good, just as it is," Kurt replied. He grabbed the key to the room and opened the door. "After you." He waved her forward.

Emily stepped into the corridor and Kurt spanked her ass when she walked past him. She smiled and thought how she couldn't wait to get him back in their room.

CHAPTER 5

T he warbling staccato of Colton's half drank glass of water vibrating on the end table where he'd left it yanked him from his sleep. "Shit," he muttered, rubbing his eyes. No good. There was far too much work to be done for him to be dozing off now. Standing in the long boarding line, breathing in all the stale, stifling air while amongst the throng of his fellow passengers awaiting boarding had really drained him.

Don't forget the booze, buddy. Pretty sure that had more to do with you passing out than waiting in a damn line. You just couldn't help yourself. Hold it together!

He crossed the cabin and entered the small bathroom, looked in the mirror, and sighed. Bags under his eyes, thinning, dark hair disheveled from the nap. He looked more like a vagrant than the rich investor he was posing as.

If he was going to mingle and not draw attention to himself, he'd need to clean himself up before heading out and stop wasting more time *not* doing his job. Colton turned on the shower and stripped down, waiting a minute or so for the water to warm up. He checked himself out in the mirror once more. He was no longer the twenty-four-year-old go-getter he once was, but he was no slouch, either. A granite jaw, chiseled pecs, and broad shoulders. An athletic build tapering down to a V-shape at the waist. A mixture of good genetics and hard work kept his body in a condition other men would kill for. But for Colton, it was more about being a well-oiled machine, ready to perform the job, whatever that may be. An unprepared marshal quickly became a dead marshal.

But lately he'd been ruining those good habits with bad habits. Chiefly, his worsening alcoholism. How long until he could no longer perform the job?

Steam filled the room, and Colton stepped into the piping-hot water.

The heat didn't bother him; he thrived in it.

<hr>

COLTON STEPPED out of his cabin and looked around. It was early evening and the hustle and bustle of the occupants heading toward the common area cars was an annoyance he'd have to find a way to work through. Being able to operate with minimal distractions would be ideal, but every job was different, and you had to do your best work in whatever conditions the job demanded. His first task would simply be to be around as many of his fellow passengers as possible, gather whatever intel he could. Maybe, if he was lucky, he'd get something solid, or at least a hunch about someone. Sometimes all it took was a feeling, some idea that *maybe* that person was off that led to further digging, and with luck, a break in the case. Colton wasn't so sure the Rail Car Cleaver case would be so simple. The nature of the train itself meant that damn near every passenger was going to feel *off*. Everyone here was under a false name, thus by default they were likely to give odd vibes.

The bar was about as good a place as any to people watch and do some digging. Colton stretched his head to the side, trying to look at the car map posted on the wall behind a hard plastic cover. The couple blocking his way moved. The man looked at Colton. "Excuse me works," he said.

"Mmm," Colton replied. He'd only been waiting for them to move, rather than inconvenience them, but as one might expect, the clientele aboard the train were likely to be assholes. He wasn't in the mood to deal with snobby pricks. His fuse had been half lit since the moment he boarded, the strain of the undercover assignment taking its toll already.

Is it the assignment? Or is it your crumbling mental state and inability to leave your vices home?

He pushed the train of thought aside. Self-examinations had no place mid-assignment. Even if he'd concluded the strain of the job, and his ever-worsening alcoholism, compromised his ability to complete the mission, it was too late. There was no replacement ready to go, no way to take him off the case until the train ride was over, and by that point, if he didn't do his job properly, a lot of people could die.

The bar was several cars away, only a few minutes' walk, even while dipping and dodging through the throng of people milling about.

Making his way through the train, Colton couldn't help but appreciate the design. The attention to detail was top-notch. Nothing looked cheap, and the entire train so far *felt* as if it was larger than it was. Credit to the interior designers, and the team in charge of the layout.

Entering the bar, Colton gave a cursory glance of his surroundings before taking a seat next to a large gentleman sporting a chrome dome and a trimmed white goatee. He wore a black suit, and though Colton hadn't the slightest idea of the brand, he could tell it cost an exorbitant amount of money.

Though the interior design did an excellent job making the space feel larger, the crowd of people in the area worked against the illusion and Colton felt the walls around him closing in. He hated tight enclosures and crowds. Anywhere he wasn't in complete control with an unimpeded view of the entries and exits bothered him. Another recently developed problem he'd kept hidden from the staff psychologists.

A drink would calm his nerves and quell the growing static creeping up in his brain. Since the onset of the issue, he'd been able to keep it at bay and prevent it from affecting him in the line of duty. Compartmentalization was something Colton had mastered years ago, but something about the mission had him on edge, and he worried if he'd be able to keep it together this time. He motioned to the bartender, a pretty, young woman wearing the same black pants, white long sleeve shirt, black vest combo much of the staff wore. She smiled. "What can I do for you, sir?" she said.

"I'll take a Jack and Coke," Colton said, and nodding at the gentleman next to him, he added, "and get this man another of whatever he is drinking, please."

"Right away. Oh, and my name is Jennifer, if you need me." She turned around and prepared the drinks.

The large man placed his hand on Colton's. "You wouldn't be trying to fuck me, would you?" he asked.

Colton pulled his hand from underneath the man's bear paw. "No, I was just hoping for some conversation. I'm here alone and I've never done anything like this before. I don't know what to expect. Just trying to find good conversation tonight."

Smiling, the man replied, "Well, there's one thing you did right," he said, leaning closer. "Plenty of the people here are looking to spice up their lives a bit, rekindle the spark with their loved ones. Stupid, if you ask me. Then there are the ones who come here to indulge together, think outside the box, if you will. Those people, they're on the right track. You can do a lot more than fuck your wife here, if you're so inclined. You just need to be ready to pony up the cash. But the real smart ones, they come here alone. You can do *anything*."

Jennifer returned with the drinks and placed them in front of both men. Colton sipped the Jack and Coke, while the large man threw back the shot of tequila.

"I'm Sam, by the way," Colton said, giving the man his fake name. "What did you say yours was?"

"I didn't. And I won't. I like to remain anonymous. Look, Sam, I realize I might have come off a bit rude earlier when I asked if you were trying to fuck me." He leaned back in his seat, allowing Colton to see the large-breasted blonde sitting next to him. "I meant nothing by it. Actually, I was thinking maybe you wanted to have fun with my friend here. The perks of riding the train stag."

Colton shook his head, laughing. "No, I'm all set. I appreciate the offer, though."

The man winked. "Alright, but don't say I never tried to do you any favors. A spit roast can be a hell of a good time." He stood up and the woman next to him followed. As they made to leave the bar, the man placed a beefy hand on Colton's shoulder. "I'll see you around, Sam."

Colton looked at the perfectly manicured hands. There were dark stains under his fingernails. He hadn't realized he spaced out staring at the man's fingers until the stranger repeated himself, louder.

"Sorry, I zoned out. What did you say?"

"I said, I'll see you around, Sam."

"Ah. Sure, ok. Maybe we can have some fun later."

"I bet we will," the man said as he exited the bar, leading the blonde by the hand.

There was something off about that man, Colton couldn't say what, but he was one to keep an eye on for sure. The first person he'd spoken to and already he was getting bad vibes. This mission was going to be even tougher than he'd anticipated.

William Crandall escorted the beautiful woman from the bar, his long strides making it difficult for her to keep up. He pulled at her, making sure she didn't lag too far behind. What a wonderful idea. When word had first gotten his way about the train, he was skeptical. A hedonistic train where everyone traveled under assumed identities, with proprietors so rich they were able to sweep any problem under the rug.

Sure, the wild sex was the reason most people were on the train, but from the whispers William had heard, *anything* was possible. Theft, assault, rape, murder. As long as you could pony up, any crime could be *covered up.* The rich knew how to indulge and made the crimes of the poor look meek in comparison. Take pedophiles, for example. The everyday pedo might harm a few kids, get caught and go to jail. The elite? They made lifestyles out of it. Defiling innocent lives, debasing them. He'd heard stories of cannibalism. All sorts of crazy shit. Could you really do that here? Pedophilia and cannibalism weren't things that excited William. That shit was disgusting. But the prospect of anything goes? Of doing what-ever you wanted without fear of getting caught? Now that was an idea that excited him.

But here? On the train? He wouldn't get caught, but his deeds would be discovered. He would make sure of that much. In fact, it was the entire point of him being here. Daddy might not have been around when William was a child, but the man's money had a way of opening doors and using the old prick's money to ride the Coastal Express might turn out to be the best decision he'd ever make.

Infamy.

He flashed the keycard against the door; it beeped. William entered the room, the blonde shut the door behind him. She stood on her toes and wrapped her arms around his neck, craning up for a kiss. William pushed the top of her head down, forcefully guiding her where he wanted.

"Right to business," she said.

"Pleasure first, then business," William replied as he slid his pants down, his large cock erect and throbbing.

The woman ran her tongue along his shaft, locked eyes with him, and wrapped her lips around him. She started slowly at first, focusing on the head, swirling her tongue around it. William groaned, and as if it were her cue, she took him deeper into her mouth, moving back and forth with a rhythmic motion, using her hand to pump the lower part of the shaft. She turned her wrist while pumping and sucking and the feeling was almost too much. William tossed his head back in ecstasy.

"Fuccckkk," he grunted. He hadn't even gotten her name, but that didn't stop her from giving him the best blowjob he'd ever had. He felt a warm, tingling sensation in his balls, a pressure building up, until the dam was ready to burst. William grabbed her by the head, digging his fingers into the back of her skull. He felt his penis hit the back of her throat, but she didn't fight it. Instead, the woman swirled her tongue as best she could, given the mouthful she had, and gripped his ass cheeks.

Thick, warm jets of cum pumped from his cock, skipping her tongue and going straight to the back of her throat. He cried out in ecstasy, his legs trembling.

When William finished cumming, she pulled back, a mixture of saliva and semen dripping from her lips.

No gag reflex on her, he thought, staring at the gross mixture in her mouth. She'd swallowed, but the act of deepthroating had forced stomach bile up her esophagus, though she'd managed to not puke.

William reached down and pulled his pants up. The woman stood and crossed the room, lying flat on her back. She pulled her short skirt up and spread her legs, running a finger along her glistening slit. "My turn," she said.

"Oh, it's your turn, all right," he said, opening the closet door. He reached in and retrieved a huge meat cleaver.

"What the fuck is that for?" the woman asked, her eyes widening.

William smiled. He stalked forward, licking his lips, gripping the cleaver. A lion creeping toward its prey.

The woman screamed, spittle and sperm flying from her mouth. There was no place for her to run, her back against the wall.

The overhead light glinted off the cleaver as he swung.

She tried to get up and run but couldn't dodge the heavy swing in time. The cleaver connected just above her elbow, slicing through flesh, muscle, and bone. William yanked it back, and the woman screamed again, this time in pain rather than fear. The swing had almost severed her arm. A few sinewy threads of meat held the dangling appendage in place. Blood spewed from the wound, a river of crimson spilling forth.

William swung again, striking the same spot and severing the arm. He followed through with the swing, letting the blade continue its path until it sunk into her side with a meaty whack.

He pulled and grunted; the cleaver stuck. He grabbed her by the collar of her dress and tossed her to the floor like a rag doll. She cried out in pain and crawled toward the door, blood squirting behind her, leaving a snail trail in her wake. He took two long strides and stomped on her foot, shattering the woman's ankle.

The massive loss of blood had already weakened her to the point where she could offer no resistance. She cried and waited for him to finish the job.

William placed a foot on her back, gripped the handle and pulled, ripping the cleaver free as blood sprayed from the gouge in her side, painting the walls of the cabin with her blood.

He swung again and again, chopping away as blood flew every which way, covering him with flecks of bone and viscera. A soupy mess of internal organs and bodily fluid pooled in the center of her body, which now looked more like raw hamburger than human flesh.

William thought about calling for a cleanup but decided against it. Not because he wanted to sleep in the mess he'd created in the room, but rather he wanted this to be just one more of the many that would be discovered. If infamy was the goal, it wouldn't help to have the train's proprietors cleaning up after him. And, if he were honest, he wasn't one-hundred percent sure he trusted the rumors he'd heard. If he were going to test them out, doing so at the end of the trip made more sense than the beginning. At least that way he could kill his way out or plot an escape if the rumors didn't pan out. He would continue creating more carnage, adding to the body count, and when this ride was all said and done, the Rail Car Cleaver would go down as the most notorious serial killer in history.

He stepped over the woman's entrails, shoes squelching in the blood. In the bathroom, he turned the shower on and stripped naked. The woman had revitalized him. Once he washed up, he would begin the hunt once more.

<h1 style="text-align:center">Chapter 6</h1>

Kurt sat at the small table in the dining car with Emily casting flirtatious grins, not only at him, but at other men who lingered nearby. Normally such a thing would spark jealousy in him, igniting the primal urge to bash someone's face in, but being here with Emily and knowing the mind-blowing sex they'd had not long ago, and the promise of more, his jealousy abated. A part of him knew if he let her get more comfortable and encouraged her newfound sexual awakening, it might lead to fun things down the road. He wasn't sure about the glances at other men, but maybe he could convince her to bring another woman into the bed. He'd seen plenty of threesomes in porn he'd rented from the video store and thought maybe it would be fun to try. But he knew it had to be a woman. He couldn't stand to see Emily with another man. The image in his mind alone was driving him ballistic.

The dining car was lined with the same mahogany wood as their cabin. Plush red velvet chairs and the same red carpet adorned the room. Gold accented mirrors lined one wall and servers passed among the seated passengers attending to their every need.

"Isn't this the most glorious thing you've ever seen?" Emily asked.

Kurt sipped his drink and set the glass down. "It's the second best, after you."

Emily blushed and batted her eyes at him.

Whatever has gotten into her, I'd like it to stick around a while, he thought. Here on the train, he felt a complete abandonment from the world around them. No stress, no worries about his job, just him and Emily doing whatever they want, whenever they want. It was a liberating feeling made more comfortable by the never-ending drinks the server continued to bring. He couldn't remember his glass getting anywhere past half-empty.

Emily stuffed a shrimp in her mouth, and he smiled. It was perfect.

Several drinks later, Kurt's vision blurred, and the swaying motion of the train played tricks with his head. It felt like it was lurching from one side to the other, and it didn't take long for him to struggle to simply stay upright.

"Kurt, hon, are you ok?" Emily asked. She reached a hand across the table and rested it gently on his.

"I...don...feel..." Kurt never finished the sentence. His stomach churned, felt like it flipped upside down, and then he vomited all over the table. Red chunky remnants of his seafood lasagna hit the table and splattered on him and Emily. Viscous strands of puke spilled over the sides of the table. He wretched again, unable to control himself, and this time he puked all over Emily's plate of shrimp. He puked so forcefully it almost drowned out the horrified gasps from the surrounding tables.

Kurt's mind reeled and his throat burned from both the acidic stomach bile and the force at which he had thrown up. The train swayed again, and once more he tossed chunks. A mouthful of noodles and sauce mixed with bourbon forcefully escaped his mouth. The soupy liquid extinguished the small candle in the center of the table. Feeling weak, Kurt didn't understand how he possibly had so much food and liquid inside of him. He prayed for an end to the madness. Prayer seemed to be the only option because, so far, he had been unable to control his body.

To his side, a woman couldn't hold in her revulsion any longer and she too vomited, further adding to the stench of puke. Her partner pushed out of his seat in disgust.

Emily mimicked the man, knocking her chair to the ground as she shot up. Her outfit, now stained red and orange by chunks of pasta and chewed fish, clung to her hair and face.

"Kurt!" she screamed. She held her arms out, staring in disbelief at the disgusting scene.

Kurt wanted to reply, but he knew the moment he'd open his mouth, more vomit would follow. His stomach churned and another stream of puke shot up his esophagus, this time with less force, and less volume. He was able to keep the floodgates closed and swallowed it. His throat was so raw he almost didn't feel the burning sensation as he gutted the puke.

"Kurt, are you fucking kidding me? Did you drink too much? I told you to slow down," Emily said. He was vaguely aware of her arm around his shoulder. He couldn't tell if she was pissed off or concerned. Not that it mattered much, because at the moment it was taking his full concentration to keep from throwing up once more. He would worry about her feelings later.

The train shook, and that was all it took for Kurt lose his focus. He burped, and another stream came out. Strands of saliva hung from his mouth, stretching down to his lap. A noodle dangled from his nostril.

Emily let go of him and backed up. Snot bubbles escaped his nose, and the noodle plopped to the ground. Kurt felt like he was about to pass out. Maybe he was dying. At least he wouldn't be able to puke if he were dead.

Amidst the gasps and murmurs from the other passengers, Kurt was vaguely aware of a commotion. Soon, two members of the train's staff were at his side, lifting him from the vomit-soaked chair, the red velvet slick with puke.

"Come with us," one of them said. Kurt didn't respond. Didn't care who they were or what they wanted. He just wanted his stomach to stop betraying him.

The room went by in a blur as the men dragged him out of the dining car like he was a petulant child. Emily followed, but at a distance. She was trying not to get more puke on her clothes and was careful not to put her hands in the chunks already on her.

"Where are you taking him?" Emily asked. Kurt, drunk and confused, hardly recognized her voice and made no move to resist. It took everything in him to simply remain conscious.

The men readjusted their grips, grasping under his armpits and digging in with no regard to the pain their rough grip caused.

"Ma'am, he needs to go to the infirmary. He'll be well taken care of there," one of the men said. "It would be best if you went to your cabin to clean up. We will bring him back as soon as he's better. Our on-board physician will evaluate and treat him."

The man spoke softly to his companion who let out a groan. The second man then dug into Kurt's vomit coated pants pocket and fished out his cabin key, then handed it to Emily. "You'll need this, ma'am," he said.

Kurt lifted his head and noticed tears running down Emily's cheeks. Her clothes were stained badly as though she were painted in puke. A moment of clarity sliced through the haze of nausea, and he felt guilty for putting Emily through this. He didn't think he'd had too much to drink. Certainly not enough to be on the verge of passing out. Another flip of his stomach pushed all other thoughts aside, and he struggled to hold on and not throw up again. The last thing he remembered before being stuffed into a bright white room was a large, bald man walking by the door, and then the doctor entering the infirmary, closing the door behind him.

Blackness swarmed his vision, and he knew nothing else.

EMILY STUMBLED back to the cabin. Kurt's puke had started to cool against her skin. It was thick and soaked through the cotton shirt, making it stick to her. She unlocked the door and hurried inside, closing the door and leaning against it, trying not to cry again.

It had been a long time since Kurt had gotten that sick from drinking before, and she couldn't remember it having that effect on him the times he *did.* She didn't think he had that many drinks, but maybe she was mistaken. She'd had a few herself and wasn't paying attention to Kurt's intake.

The stench of vomit assaulted her nostrils, and Emily felt her own stomach respond to the foul stench. She stripped out of her clothes and kicked them into a pile by the door.

Setting the key on a small table near the couch, she slipped into the shower, turned on the water, and once the temperature was warm enough, stepped inside.

The cascading hot water tingled her skin. She soaked her hair and stood under the running water, letting the chunks of regurgitated food wash off her. At her feet, the sauce colored water ran along the bottom of the tub, circling the drain before disappearing. A few chunks of food collected on top of the drain; the small circles not large enough to accommodate the bigger chunks of Kurt's dinner. She ignored the chunks as best she could, squirting a handful of shampoo into her hand, then running it through her long red hair. The lavender scent helped to mask the scent of vomit in the bathroom. With any luck, the smell would come out of her hair, too.

After a bit of time, the shower became a gratifying relief from the revolting scene at dinner. She welcomed the water and soap, lathering up her entire body twice to make sure she didn't miss anything.

Emily dried up, and with a towel wrapped around her body and a second wrapped around her hair, stepped into the main area to retrieve the soiled clothes. She gasped; eyes locked at the foot of the door where she'd undressed. The clothes were missing, no trace of them or vomit chunks. All that remained was a faint, lingering scent of vomit. She glanced toward the little table where she'd left the room key. It was sitting right where she'd left it.

What the fuck? she thought. *How did someone get into our room? And why would they take my nasty clothes?* A shiver ran through her at the realization unbeknownst to her, a stranger entered the room while she was naked in the shower. What if they had seen her? What if the person was a sexual deviant and had come after her while she was in the shower? A dark feeling settled inside her gut, and she wrapped her arms around herself. She hoped it was something as simple as room service trying to be helpful, but truthfully, she wasn't sure what to think. As much as she hated the idea of room service entering the room while she was in the shower, the other possibilities were far worse.

CHAPTER 7

No leads, no actionable intel. The evening so far had been a monumental failure. But failure wasn't an option for Colton. The word simply did not exist in his lexicon. Failure was something lesser marshals accepted.

Colton may be slipping, may be an alcoholic, but he still thought of himself as a cut above the rest, even with his problems. He needed to take down the Cleaver before he had a train full of bodies on his hands. Though he had found no evidence the man was here aside from the anonymous call, he was sure of it. His gut had never steered him wrong in the past.

Something was not right aboard the Coastal Express. Colton intended on getting to the bottom of it.

The bald man was one lead, the only lead, really. And it wasn't much of a lead, if he was being honest. All he had to go on was a hunch. But sometimes that's how it went. You play the cards in your hand, and if those cards amounted to shit? Well, then you started making it up as you go. Colton wondered if he should have accepted the man's offer to head back to his room. It would have gotten him closer to the bald man and he would have been able to have a little fun doing it. Kill two birds with one stone. But he knew it was the wrong way to get the job done. He was a professional, and though his fellow travelers may be here for sex and uninhibited desires, he was not.

The department had to know you'd find yourself in situations like that. Besides, it's for the mission. The mission takes priority. And it would be fun. Colton pushed the thought away. He was becoming a jaded marshal, which was no good.

Things had been interesting since he'd gotten to the bar, at least. As he sipped his drink alone, watching his surroundings, there had been a commotion in the dining car adjacent to the bar. When the dust settled, it had turned out to be nothing more than a passenger who'd been unable to handle his alcohol, puking all over his date. A few other passengers had joined the party once the chunks started flying, adding their own partially digested stomach contents to the equation. Thinking about it again, Colton snorted. *Guess he isn't getting laid tonight, poor sap.*

He turned his head in time to see a woman sidle up to him, the side of her breasts grazing him as she sat on the stool. She flashed a smile at him, her perfectly shaped teeth brilliantly white and dazzling. The woman had long, beautifully thick auburn hair. It framed her head like a lion's mane and flowed down her back.

"I'm Arianna," she said, "but you can call me Ari."

"Is that your real name, Ari, or is that your name for the trip?" Colton said.

"Does it matter?"

"No, it doesn't. I'm not sure why I asked. I've never done something like this before," he laughed. "I'm Sam."

"Are you though?" she asked, flashing a smile again.

"Am I what?" Colton asked.

She sighed. "Are you Sam, I meant. Like, is that your real name? I was trying to be funny, you know? You asked if I was really Arianna, and so I asked if you were really Sam. Not much for social cues, huh?"

Colton's face went red. She was right. He often buried himself in his work, leaving little time for him to socialize. All his free time after working hours typically was spent on whatever assignments he was working, and lately, capping the night with a bottle. Colton was a marshal, 24/7, for better and for worse. He wondered if his lack of social life, and experience talking to people outside of work, would lead him to botch this assignment.

"Sorry, I don't get out much. I bury myself in my job, and all that, ya know?" he said, choosing to be honest, while remaining vague. It was easier than carrying on another lie.

"I can respect that. How about you buy me a drink and I'll teach you all about social interaction," Arianna said, placing a hand on his thigh.

Colton felt a stirring in his pants. While he wouldn't let this go as far as she seemed appeared to want, he wasn't opposed to having a few more drinks with the woman. That would allow him to dig for information from her, and if she had nothing to contribute to the investigation, it would allow him to hide in plain sight, gleaning whatever he could from the other passengers. Someone *had* to know something. About the Cleaver, about the sleepers, about the mysterious proprietors, Boulder and Smith.

Colton signaled the bartender. She brought a Jack and Coke for Colton, and took Arianna's order, a martini.

"For someone who doesn't get out much, the bartender already seems to know what you like, and we haven't even been here for twenty-four hours yet," Arianna said.

"I've been here for a little while now. Got bored just sitting around in my room."

"Mmm. And what are you doing, spending all your time at the bar?"

"Searching for someone," Colton said, with a hint of sexual suggestion. Another true statement, this time with a misleading tone.

Arianna licked her lips. "No wedding ring?" she asked, leaning closer so Colton could feel her breath in his ear. "I think I know what you're looking for."

"I guess we'll find out, now, won't we?" And he would find out. She either had the information he needed, or she didn't. He'd string her along, let her think he was looking for a wet hole to stick his dick in, so long as playing the game allowed him to fish for information. If she had nothing to give, well then, he'd end the conversation and let her continue her quest to find a plaything.

The bartender brought Arianna's martini over. She thanked the woman with a nod of the head and turned her attention back to Colton. "So, Sam," she said, "what do you do for work?"

"I dabble. Gathering and acquiring things for my employer. Really just depends. Each job is different," Colton said.

"So, you do contract work?"

"Something like that."

"Secretive, huh?"

Colton laughed. "Isn't that the point of this trip? So, we can have some fun and keep our secrets."

"You're right, Sam. But sometimes sharing is fun, isn't it?" She winked.

"It can be, if you share the right things. I'm just trying to figure out who's gonna share what I want."

"I like to share, Sam."

"Well, we're talking right now. Let's drink our drinks and see what happens, ok. I'm very…specific in my wants. You may not be willing to share what I'm looking for." Sam winked.

Arianna sighed. Clearly, she was getting bored with Colton's game, though in her mind they were playing a sex game, and in his, he was playing a game of fishing for knowledge. "Yeah, ok, so talk. What do you want to talk about? You seem different than the others on this train, but I can't put my finger on it. A lot of rich eccentric types here. I guess that's the point, but you seem more… reserved than the rest of these dudes. And to be honest, you look like you know how to handle yourself," she said, eyeing Colton's chiseled physique through his clothes.

Colton ignored the compliment. He was thrown off his game for a second. How easily Arianna had pegged him as different. Was she that good? Or was he losing his touch? Maybe both. "I don't know about different; we all are a bit odd. Otherwise, why would we be here? Truthfully, I've heard things can get wild out there, on this train. I think I'm looking for more than you've got."

"People are into all sorts of things. I haven't heard anything specific here, just that you can get away with pretty much anything, if you've got the money to keep it quiet. What that means, I'm not so sure."

"What do you mean by *anything*?" Colton asked. He already knew what she meant, but he wanted to hear it from someone else.

Colton was trying his best with his questioning but was finding it difficult to get the intel he needed without giving himself away. This was no normal mission, and its difficulties were already threatening to blow his cover, and the case.

"I guess I'll spell this out for you. Sam, you really need to learn context clues. Did you skip that lesson in class? It applies to speech, too. Not just writing. I mean anything. If you have enough money, you can quite literally get away with murder on this train. Everyone is under an assumed identity. There are no cameras anywhere. None of us were here. Anything you want can be swept under the rug, so long as you pony up. That's why the elite love this. They are free to do all the sick shit they usually do at home, in a setting where someone else will clean up the mess. You go a bit hard on the BDSM, kill your partner? It goes away. You're one of those pedo freaks? It goes away. You like a little torture, murder, rape? As long as you can pay, it goes away."

So, the rumors were true. That would make finding the Rail Car Cleaver harder than I'd already figured it would be, Colton thought. If that was the type of shit the elites on this train were into, he could be anyone.

"Wow, that's a bit… much, don't you think?" Colton asked.

"Is it? People with money can do whatever they want. They always have and they always *will*."

"And the owners are ok with it? Do you know anything about them? What do you know about Boulder and Smith?"

He really hoped he wasn't pushing too much. Hoped the question didn't betray his true occupation.

"I wouldn't say I know anything about those two, because I don't. But I will say that I'm smart enough to know that two people who have enough money to build *this*," she said, making a sweeping gesture, "are not the people you want to go asking questions about. Especially not when you're on their property. And definitely not when I just told you these guys can sweep murder under the rug. Whatever they are into, I'm sure I don't want to know about it."

Colton bit his lip, nodded in silent agreement. She was right.

"You know, Sam, you might want to be careful who you talk to around here. Plenty of people are here to drink and fuck, but you're asking an awful lot of prying things that might get *you* swept under the rug, if word gets out."

Colton swallowed his drink. "Yeah, you're right. Maybe I should just stick to getting laid. Worry about that stuff when I'm home safe."

Arianna finished her martini, spun on the seat to face Colton, spreading her legs as she did. Under her tight dress, she wore no panties, and Colton got a front row view of her glistening slit. She cleared her throat, breaking his trance. Colton looked into her eyes and she grinned at him. He watched in awe as she moved her hand between her legs, stuck a finger in her pussy, brought the hand to her face, and sucked the finger.

The bulge in his pants was about to explode. The mission was all but forgotten as the primal urge to orgasm took control of his mind and body.

Until the bald man from earlier walked by, nodding his head at Colton.

He was alone, the beautiful woman he'd invited Colton to fuck with him, gone. *That doesn't mean anything, right?* Colton asked himself, momentarily more concerned with the woman in front of him than the mission. But when he remembered the dark stains under the man's nails, the professional in him wrestled control of his mind and body away from the head between his thighs.

Colton slid off his seat without saying another word to Arianna. She mumbled something but he ignored her. She'd be fine without him.

But the woman who'd been with the bald man? Maybe she was fine, but Colton's gut told him otherwise. He needed to find out.

FINDING the room turned out to be more difficult than he had thought. He'd watched the man earlier and had a good idea of its general area, but someone had passed in front of his line of sight, obstructing his vision long enough that he'd missed which room they'd ducked into. If his gut feeling had been as strong about the bald man earlier, he'd have never let the man slip away. Or maybe if he had been on top of his game. No matter, Colton thought he'd still be able to find the room, it would just take a bit more time. There was no way to sneak his way into the rooms, so far as he could tell, and the sound-proofing was truly immaculate. Anybody could be in any room, doing who the hell knew what. Colton figured the best way to proceed would be to simply knock on as many doors as possible, see who answers, and eliminate them from the list of possibilities. If an upset passenger opened the door, he'd simply apologize and act as if he'd forgotten where his room was. This would also allow him to potentially whittle the list of possible suspects down, and maybe he could find a way to snag the master key and do a few *wellness checks.* Get in, get out, and replace the key before he was found out.

He got to work, knocking on doors and taking a lay of the land. Even if he couldn't find the man's room right off the bat, assigning faces to rooms might help him later on if his pursuit of the bald man turned out to be for naught. Still, it was awkward. In his line of work, he'd seen plenty of nudity, but he was surprised how many men and women answered the door in the nude. He knew it was a *hedonistic* getaway, but he hadn't expected to interrupt so many sex sessions. Opening the door with your meat at full hog, glistening with your partner's juices, was certainly a choice. One he wouldn't have made, had the shoe been on the other foot.

Of the rooms he'd considered as possibly belonging to the bald man, there had been only two he had not been able to rouse the occupants. It was possible neither of them belonged to the bald man, but with how quickly he'd disappeared earlier, Colton thought it unlikely.

But how to get the master key? The staff surely wouldn't open the door for just anyone, and he couldn't reveal his identity while undercover. The more Colton thought about it, he wasn't sure how he would even apprehend the Rail Car Cleaver once he found him. If the things he'd heard about crimes being swept under the rug held any modicum of truth, breaking his cover even to take the man into custody could be the end of the line for him.

But he couldn't allow himself to dwell on that. It was a distraction, just another intrusive thought that if allowed to fester, would put the mission in jeopardy. He'd push it out of his mind and cross that road when he came to it. One thing he knew for sure, to proceed, he needed to get a master key and see if any of the rooms belonged to the bald man.

An idea struck him. It was risky, but the only idea Colton thought might work.

He'd have to go hands on, and he'd risk breaking his cover. Colton couldn't think of a better way. He had to go with his gut feeling.

The large men who were posing as staff members, but likely doubled as security, judging by their size, had the keys. He wasn't one hundred percent sure, but those were the guys escorting boarding passengers to their rooms, and he assumed they'd all received the same spiel as he did.

Step one: Find one of the staff members and pretend he'd left his key in his room.

Step two: Subdue the man, take the key, and search the rooms.

Step two sure as shit would promise to be interesting. Colton was suddenly thankful he'd kept his body a well-oiled machine. Many of his coworkers eventually became lazy and let themselves go. Not Colton. Though he did wish he'd managed to keep the alcohol use to a minimum. No use crying over something you couldn't take back.

Colton backtracked. He'd cross the bar and make his way toward his room. Once he was close, he'd find someone to open the door for him. From that point on, he had to assume it was balls to the wall until the investigation was closed, or a member of the Coastal Express's goon squad took him out.

COLTON STOOD next to one of the staff members, waiting for the man to open his door. He'd wasted quite a bit of time tracking down one he thought he was most likely to gain the upper hand on. He would only get one shot at this, and picking the target least likely to kill him was a must. He'd scoured the cars until he found his man. Tall and muscular like the rest, but this particular goon didn't carry himself with the same dignity as the others. Complacent was the word that came to Colton's mind. Where the rest of the train's goon squad looked well-kept and organized, Colton's man appeared to be the opposite. Long, unruly hair that looked as if he hadn't showered or brushed in some time. A shaggy beard that appeared to have food crumbs stuck in it. If there was *one* member of the security team that was most likely to *not* take the job seriously, this was the guy.

The man dug through pockets of his wrinkly black pants, searching for the keycard. "Where the hell is it?" he said. "I know I just had the damn thing."

"Should I grab someone else? I don't want to be a bother."

"A bit late for that, huh?" The man continued patting himself down.

Colton was sure he'd picked the right man. This guy was a damned soup sandwich.

Mr. Complacent fished the card from the breast pocket of his vest. "I knew it was here! Now, you know this is gonna cost ya, right? The company is gonna charge your room one hundred dollars for use of the master key. If you can't find your key, a replacement will be issued, and you will be charged another one hundred dollars each day the card is missing."

"What? How does that pricing even make sense? That's fucking nuts. Have you lost your damn mind?"

"Not my rule, chief. But if you're on this train, hundreds of dollars really don't mean shit to you, now do they?"

"It isn't the money, it's the point."

"Exactly. The point is the owners don't want you losing your fucking key, yet here we are, with you somehow losing your key already. You want me to open the door or not?"

"I don't see any other choice. Open the door," Colton said.

The man swiped the card. The card reader flashed green and beeped. He stepped aside and swept his arm, gesturing to the open door.

Colton hoped the man would enter the room, it would be easier to take him by surprise from behind, but clearly, he had no intention of doing so. Colton would have to make it up on the fly. He walked into his room and started to thank the man, but stopped mid-sentence, gasped, and said, "What the hell happened to my bathroom?"

"What?" the man said, entering the room.

Colton pointed toward the bathroom. "It's a mess!"

"I don't…"

He didn't get a chance to finish the sentence. Colton picked a vase off the side table and smashed it against the man's skull. It shattered, pieces of glass flying everywhere. Blood trickled from the man's head, but he didn't go down.

Of course, this can't be easy.

The man turned around and swung wildly. Colton ducked the punch and retaliated with his own left hook to the man's rib cage. Colton tried following up with another punch, but despite his previous complacent appearance, the goon was much quicker than Colton had anticipated. He lowered his head and charged forward, narrowly avoiding Colton's strike. The man's shoulder drove into Colton's mid-section, and he wrapped both arms around Colton's waist, pivoted, and threw his body weight backward, suplexing Colton.

Oof. The air rushed from Colton's lungs. The man scrambled on top of Colton and mounted him. Colton caught his breath, trying to remain calm as he focused on defending as the large goon threw heavy punch after heavy punch. Colton dodged and blocked the blows, but still the strength behind the ones that *did* land, hurt. He needed to do something, and quickly.

The man lifted both hands above his head, making a club. As the hands came down, Colton rammed both of his knees upward and shot his hip to the sky. The man's momentum sent him tumbling over Colton's head, and both men quickly shot to their feet.

"I don't know what the fuck you think you're doing, but you're not leaving this room alive, pal," the man said.

Colton poked the bear, trying to get his temper flaring. "Why don't you come over here and try it, Nancy boy? I think you left your skirt in my bathroom."

The man's face turned beet red, and Colton knew insulting his masculinity was the right call. He charged Colton once more, but this time Colton anticipated it, stepping to the side and throwing a hard kick to the side of the man's knee. The knee moved one way and the shin the other. A sickening snap echoed through the soundproof room and the man dropped to the floor, clutching his ruined knee, screaming. "My leg! What did you do to my leg?" he shrieked.

"You said you were gonna kill me. I was defending myself." Colton said, pulling two pairs of zip-tie cuffs from the bed-side table drawer. "Now, I'm gonna tie you up, then I'm gonna put you to sleep for a bit. I know the walls are soundproof, but I want to make sure you're not gonna try to yell when I leave the room."

Colton flipped the man over. The excruciating pain left him unable to resist, probably fighting simply to remain conscious. Colton tied his wrists together behind his back, and with the other pair of cuffs, he tied the man's ankles together. With the goon restrained, Colton wrapped his arm around the man's neck and squeezed, cutting off circulation to his brain. This time, he did attempt to resist, though the effort was far too weak to make a difference. When the man stopped struggling, Colton released the hold—he wanted to knock him out, not kill him—and dragged him into the bathroom, leaving him on the floor next to the tub. He slipped the key from the man's breast pocket and exited the room.

CHAPTER 8

Kurt's eyes opened and his world went from black to an all-consuming, blinding white. If his head wasn't already pounding, the light would have brought on a headache like no other. "Turn it off," he croaked, his throat burning. It was raw from the vomiting and the scent of his puke was so strong it almost overpowered the bleached, sanitized smell of the infirmary.

"Ahh, you're awake," a voice said. "That is unfortunate for you. This is going to hurt."

Kurt looked around, searching for the voice. His eyes slowly adjusted to the bright light above him, letting him better take in his surroundings. The situation was dire. One minute he was puking his brains out, and the next thing he knew, he was strapped to an operating table.

The man who had spoken walked into his view and leaned over him. "I'm Dr. Hebert, not that it makes any difference. You won't be around long enough to bother committing my name to memory. It seems you won't be making the return trip."

"What do you mean?" Kurt said. "Where am I? Get my wife, please. Let her know where I am." The softly swaying motion of the train unsettled his stomach. Still drowsy, he'd hardly registered the severity of what Dr. Hebert had said to him.

Kurt saw Dr. Hebert's face wrinkle as he smiled under the surgical mask. Doctor or not, he was dressed for the part from head to toe. Kurt struggled against his restraints, but it was no good. They were cinched tight.

"Let me go!" he growled. His heart thundered in his chest, adrenaline starting to take over.

The wheels on the table squeaked as the doctor pushed Kurt to the end of the room that could only be described as sterile. When the table stopped, Kurt looked around and his focus turned to the contraption he was parked next to. Two huge cylinders, one on either side of a control panel. The cylinders appeared to be filled with some sort of dark fluid, and within the fluid, Kurt could make out something darker, though he couldn't tell what was in either tank.

Dr. Hebert snatched one of Kurt's arms and maneuvered it around while tapping the arm, searching for a vein. "This will do," Dr. Hebert said as he stuck the needle in Kurt's arm, causing Kurt to wince in pain. The man certainly made no effort to sterilize or minimize damage to Kurt's body.

"What the fuck, man? Stop it! I was only puking. I had too much to drink, that's all."

Dr. Hebert smiled. "Oh, you didn't have too much to drink. You just happened to be the unlucky chosen one of this evening."

The catheter was attached to another tube that ran directly into the cylinder behind Kurt.

Dr. Hebert dropped his arm and repeated the process to Kurt's other arm.

"Fucking stop it, now!" Kurt screamed. Thoughts raced through his mind. Where was Emily? Where was he? Were they doing this to her, too? For a moment, he concluded this was some sort of alcohol induced nightmare, but the sharp pain on his arms from the needles told him otherwise.

With both arms hooked up, Dr. Hebert walked to the panel and began clicking away. The sound of a machine whirring to life startled Kurt, and before he knew it, the clear tubes turned red as his blood filled them and ran the length to the large cylinders.

"Come on, man. Whatever you're doing, I'm begging you to stop. I didn't sign up for this shit. I didn't consent to this! Look, I can pay. Pick someone else, please. You don't need to do this." Kurt's mind clouded, and he felt confused. A side effect of whatever they'd slipped him, or rapidly losing blood. Kurt wasn't sure, but he found himself unable to escape his restraints.

Dr. Hebert spoke as Kurt's essence was funneled from his body against his will. "If it makes any consolation to you, son, you're a part of something bigger than you will ever know. Modern medicine and science have never seen something like this before. You're helping to satiate the sleepers. Helping to sustain something greater than yourself. A lot of very rich, very bad people want to get their hands on these things, and you are helping to make that possible."

Kurt screamed, a guttural sound from the depths of his very being. He struggled against the restraints but was powerless to free himself as his life was drained from his body.

"Get me the fuck out of here!" Kurt screamed.

"Oh, and son? If you think it hurts now, just wait. I'm supposed to really put you through it. Does something to the blood, or at least that's what they told me." Dr. Hebert removed his surgical mask and plucked a cigar from his pocket and put it between his teeth before removing a cigar cutter from his pocket. He held the cutter up. "This isn't for the cigar, son."

Kurt's eyes bulged from his head, and he thrashed despite the restraints. He cursed and screamed, the veins in his neck bulging.

"Don't you touch me!"

Dr. Hebert grabbed Kurt's hand and separated the pinky from the rest of the digits before placing the finger through the center of the cutter.

"No, please. Don't do it!"

"Might want to go to your happy place now, son," he said as he closed the guillotine blade over Kurt's pinky. Kurt screamed again as most of the finger separated and blood squirted from the wound. Dr. Hebert gripped the pinky, hanging on by strands of bloodied tissue and bone, and began to work the digit side to side until it snapped off like a wishbone. Kurt howled louder.

"I always wanted to try that," Dr. Hebert smiled. "But I think we're gonna have to use something else for the rest." He tossed the cigar cutter aside and retrieved a pair of bone shears from a drawer, holding them up. He smiled as the overhead lights glinted off the edge of the polished surgical tool. "These should do the trick, but first, we need to cauterize the wound. Can't waste all that blood."

Kurt cried out for Emily and Dr. Hebert laughed.

CHAPTER 9

Colton had his small Smith & Wesson Model 38 in one hand, and the master key in the other, readying himself to pop into the room and make a quick check. He silently cursed the task force's intel. Clearly, they'd fucked up and hadn't done due diligence, because nobody had bothered to tell him he was aboard a train where literally anything goes, so long as you could pay the tab to clean it up. That included murder. Jesus Christ, what kind of insanity was this? How deep did the well go? Hell, he might be the least armed person on the train if that was common knowledge to the rest of the passengers. If he'd have known, certainly he would have selected a bigger piece, and probably would have brought a few. Sure, the little guy was still a gun, and a well-placed bullet could get the job done, but there were guns that performed better, and were more practical for situations where stealth wasn't a priority. Not that he was in such a position yet, but conceivably, if this mission goes to shit, he might be there, and need something with more stopping power and a larger clip.

Colton swiped the card. The door beeped. He pushed it in and followed closely behind, gun raised and ready to shoot.

"Fuck me daddy, fuck me daddy," cried a woman's voice. When the door swung open, Colton was confronted by a woman being pounded doggy style while another man stood in the corner naked, except for a metal contraption covering his penis. Both men and the woman looked up at Colton, shocked at the intrusion. The woman spoke first. "You want to fuck me in front of my husband too, big boy? Put that gun away and pull out your hammer and we can teach that cuck whose pussy this really is."

Colton's eyes widened, horrified at the scene unfolding in front of him. He wasn't sure he knew what a cuck was before, but he now had a pretty good idea. He closed the door and moved on to the next.

Standing in front of door number two, he swiped the card, pushed the door open, and entered. The door swung hard, and he rode it in, letting it hit the wall. He split the room into sections mentally and scanned them behind the sight of the gun.

Empty. But the bathroom door was closed.

He walked toward the door and gripped the handle, turned the knob, and pushed, gun still at the ready.

The door swung open.

Empty.

Two empty rooms. One left to check. If the search turned up empty, it didn't necessarily mean the rooms could be ruled out, though it did make them more likely to belong to someone else. The first room certainly could be ruled out.

Colton readied himself in front of the third room, performing the same actions. Swipe, push, enter.

The moment the door opened, before he'd even cross the threshold, he knew he'd found the one. The smell was over-powering. Carnage, blood, death. His eyes fell on what he'd already known was waiting. He stepped over through the door and into a slaughterhouse.

Blood covered every surface. The walls, the ceiling, the furniture. Colton had seen a lot of shit during his time in law enforcement. But this? This was something else.

Colton was no stranger to violent crime scenes, but this was far worse than anything he'd ever encountered. His stomach threatened to betray him, and he fought against the urge to vomit. How the hell could someone do this and leave the room in such a bloody mess? The conversation he had earlier with Ari came back to his mind and he shuddered to think how the rich could get away with such depravity. *They should all be fucking locked up*, he thought.

If this wasn't the rich, then it had to be the Cleaver. Or maybe the Rail Car Cleaver *was* one of the rich. With the things he'd learned, it made sense. Whoever it was, he'd bring the fucker to justice.

He tried his best to step around the wet spots on the carpet, but it was practically impossible. Bits and pieces of organs, intestines, bone, and meat were strewn about every-where and it was impossible to say what was what. Colton simply tried to step in spots that seemed less saturated.

The soupy mess in the middle of the room clearly belonged to a murdered human. It didn't require a degree to see that. Colton assumed the victim to be the woman he'd seen with the bald man, but there was no way to be sure. Not after what he'd learned today. The only actual proof he'd had was the woman walking off with him and not returning. His gut told him he was correct, but his gut wasn't evidence in a court of law.

And there wasn't much in the way of tangible physical evidence. Just a gelatinous soup of human remains. But there was plenty of DNA evidence, so far as Colton could tell, which luckily was admissible in court and had become increasingly common in the past few years since its introduction less than a decade ago.

Colton kept the weapon up and swung the bathroom door open.

It was empty.

But the mirror was still fogged.

The Rail Car Cleaver had been here recently, and if not him, then there was another murderer here that needed to be taken down. He groaned, thinking that his assignment just got a thousand times more complicated. He needed a fucking drink like he needed oxygen.

Colton left the room to search the train. If he was right, he knew what the Cleaver looked like. If he was wrong, he was in the same position he was now. He assumed the Cleaver didn't know who he was, yet. Hopefully that was the case, otherwise he might end up like the person in the middle of the floor.

CHAPTER 10

Emily waited nervously in her cabin for Kurt to return. At one point she poked her head out the door to speak to a passing crew member, but the man assured her that if her husband was in the infirmary, then he was receiving the best possible care. She reluctantly slunk back into the cabin and curled up on the small couch, her mind left to drift.

So much had changed in their lives, especially over the past couple of years. Their marriage used to be bulletproof, but that was shattered when Kurt cheated on her two years ago. She tried to forgive and forget, but it was the forgetting part that stymied her.

Kurt had thought that the reason she was no longer excited for sexual intimacy had to do with life's stress and general relationship malaise settling in, but the real reason Emily's sex drive had waned was that she couldn't get the image of him fucking the stupid bitch from the ad agency out of her head. When she walked in on him, grabbing the bitch's hips and pounding her ass from behind, the image seared into her brain. Now every time he wanted a blow job, all she could think about was how his dick was in another woman's ass and the thought disgusted her.

He betrayed everything at that moment.

Emily screamed at him and threw her car keys, the only thing she had on her at the time. The little whore cried out and ran from their bedroom with her clothes in her hands. Kurt tried to weasel his way out of her anger by offering shitty excuses. But what excuse could you really have for sticking your dick in another woman that wouldn't make you sound like an even bigger piece of shit?

Eventually, they worked it out and Emily gave him a second chance, mostly because she felt she had no other choice. Her parents pressured her to remain with her unfaithful husband because it was the "Godly thing" to do. They didn't believe in divorce, as evidenced by her mother staying with her father even though they all knew he'd cheated on her numerous times. Because going outside the marriage was so much *godlier* than getting a divorce? Though not a churchgoer anymore, the guilt foisted upon her brought her down mentally, and wouldn't let her escape her marriage as badly as she wanted to. Granted, things had gotten better over the past two years, but still she found herself thinking about Kurt fucking that cunt more often than she should, and it hindered her ability to truly put the past to bed and enjoy their current relationship.

And that was a major driving factor as to why she agreed to this trip to begin with. She *did* wish to work past her anger and jealousy, learn to enjoy life with her husband once more. What they did earlier was exactly what she needed. She'd let herself go and cleared her mind, focusing solely on that singular moment. It was the most freeing experience she'd had and brought with it an influx of emotions. She felt like she did when they were first married. Excited. Nervous. Bonded. They were a couple again, a partnership with each other's best interests at heart. And whether he deserved a second chance or not, Kurt *had* tried to change since that day. She hoped to continue feeling better about their relationship.

Emily sighed. She missed her husband, longed for him. She desired him physically and emotionally, yet here she was, alone again.

Several hours had passed and Emily was shaken awake by the train's movement. She didn't remember falling asleep but must've passed out while waiting for Kurt. She got up, went to the bathroom to piss, then surveyed the cabin. The waning sunlight streaming in the window clued her in that she'd slept till evening.

Where the hell is Kurt? she thought. The cabin was empty and her skin prickled. Even with Kurt's excessive puking, he should've been back by now. How long did it take to rehydrate?

It was past time to get answers. Emily slipped into a clean set of Coastal Express complimentary clothes, grabbed her card key, and headed out of her cabin.

There weren't many people out this early in the evening. No doubt many of the passengers were indulging in all kinds of sordid fantasies. A staff-member walked by, thickly built with short blonde hair.

"Excuse me," she said, gently grasping his arm. "Can you tell me where the infirmary is?"

"Sorry, ma'am. I have a dinner service to attend to." He slipped out of her grasp and glided down the hall toward the end of the car.

How could he not even be bothered to tell me where the infirmary is? she thought. She understood that secrecy was the attraction of the Coastal Express, but were the employees supposed to be pricks, too? What if she was sick? Would he have still walked away from her? She followed the man to the end of the car and entered the next.

It was another sleeper car like her own and it looked exactly the same. Three doors ahead of her on the left, a woman stepped out from her cabin.

"Excuse me," Emily said. "Can I ask you a question?"

The woman spun around with wide, bloodshot eyes. Her blonde hair was unkempt and flew around her face.

"What?" she replied, exhaling a deep breath. She was in a similar outfit to Emily, but it was stained red on the front. The woman caught Emily's stare and offered a weak smile. "Wine. I'm clumsy at times," she said, indicating her clothes.

The woman composed herself and slowed her breathing, straightening her shirt.

"What did you say again?" she asked.

"I was hoping you knew where the infirmary was. My husband got sick at dinner—"

"Oh, you were the couple in the dining car last night, right? The guy that puked everywhere," she said in a sweet southern drawl.

Emily felt her cheeks redden. "Umm, yeah, that's us. They took him to recover, and I haven't seen him since."

The woman slowly approached her, the features on her face turning from surprise to sympathy. "Hun, I wouldn't worry your pretty little head off about him. The people running this train offer the best care possible. It wouldn't do to have passengers dying on them, you know?" She winked and smiled warmly. "I bet by the time we get to Cincinnati he'll be back in your cabin and raring to go. I know I would if I was coming back to you."

Emily felt exposed under the woman's lustful gaze. She instantly crossed her arms over her chest, hoping to avoid the woman's attention.

"I don't see too many redheads on board," the woman said. She leaned closer and whispered, "is it natural?" Her eyes darted to Emily's crotch, and she felt her cheeks redden again. *Did everyone on this train just want to fuck?*

"I don't dye my hair," Emily replied.

"Hun, anytime you feel like joining in on the fun, come on here," she said, tapping the golden 53 room number. "My name's Roxy. Just let them know I said it was ok."

"Them?" Emily asked.

Roxy laughed. "Oh hun, this is your first time, isn't it?"

Emily nodded.

Roxy placed a gentle hand on her shoulder. "Just remember to say my name and you'll be fine."

"Uh, sure," Emily said. She'd lost her train of thought and didn't have anything else to say. Roxy turned from her and sashayed her way to the far end of the sleeper car until she crossed over to the next one.

Emily stood dumbfounded. How had that just happened? Did she just get propositioned to join a stranger in bed? From the sounds of it, Roxy made her think it was more than one person, too. What the hell was going on in cabin 53? She traced the numbers with a finger and then followed in the direction where Roxy headed.

Crossing into the next car, Emily found herself in the dining car. The crew must've worked hard to clean the disgusting mess Kurt had left them.

"Care for something to eat?" a uniformed employee asked. The man was older, with white hair and tanned skin. His smile reached up to his dark brown eyes.

"No, no, thank you."

"Wine or a cocktail, perhaps?"

"Maybe," Emily replied. "Can you tell me where the infirmary is? My husband got sick last night, and I haven't seen him since."

"Ah, yes. I remember it well. We haven't had to do a deep clean like that in our dining car in quite some time. Luckily our staff is used to it from the cabins. Things can get quite messy, if you know what I mean," he said with a nudge and a wink. Emily shook her head. What the hell was that supposed to mean?

"That's all fine, but the infirmary?" she asked.

"You will need permission from the conductor."

"The…sure, fine. Where can I find this person?"

"I'm afraid I can't divulge Mr. Durgin's whereabouts. He'd be quite upset with me, and I can't afford another demerit."

"All I want is to find my husband!" Emily shouted. She'd finally snapped. Between last night, the weird woman she'd run into, and the staff giving her the runaround, her patience was at an all-time low.

"Ma'am," the man said, "you would do well not to raise your voice. It's quite unbecoming."

"I don't care! Someone just give me a fucking straight answer for once."

"Ma'am," a man's voice behind her called out. "Ma'am, if you'll come with me, maybe I can help."

She spun around, ready to give the intruder an earful, and her voice caught in her throat. It was a large, bald man with a white goatee. He wore a sportscoat over a t-shirt with matching dark blue pants. He approached her, his size even more impressive up close.

"Are you the conductor? This…Durgin person?"

The man smiled. "No, ma'am, but I can be your conductor if you want. I'm just an interested bystander."

"If you know where the infirmary is, then you might be useful to me. If not, well, then I suppose we can part ways now."

"I think I can help. I'm sorry, it was a poor joke. Given the nature of our surroundings, I was trying to make you laugh. Are you sick or injured?" the large man asked. He showed genuine concern on his face, and Emily felt a little more at ease. It was relieving to hear him say he was simply telling a crude joke, something men can't help but do. She had to listen to Kurt's bullshit day in and day out.

"Much appreciated. I'm Emily. I'm looking for my husband, Kurt." She paused, worried about using her real name. It was too late now. Besides, this man was offering to help her find Kurt.

The bald man nodded and stroked his bearded chin. "William," he offered. "It's my pleasure to meet you. Now, the infirmary, you say?"

She nodded.

"Let's go see what we can find out." William guided her

toward the far exit of the dining car heading toward the sleeper cars. Emily felt relieved that she was finally getting somewhere. Hopefully, she'd find Kurt soon enough.

CHAPTER 11

William absently patted the cleaver inside his sportscoat. Stirring inside of him was a powerful desire to just butcher this woman into bite-sized chunks and to leave her bloody remains where they now stood. It took every ounce of self-control not to slaughter her right there. Had there not been any witnesses nearby, that's exactly what he'd have done. Instead, he'd play along with her stupid search in hopes that he'd get her alone.

The woman was searching for her husband, the man that had puked his guts out the night before. William was in the dining car then, trying to enjoy a nice chicken parm while scanning the other passengers for another victim. His blade needed more blood, and he was excited to get back to work.

Two tables away, the man had vomited all over the place. William watched as the crew attended to him, but also noticed that they didn't seem all that worried, either. It was sort of like they knew he'd be sick and were just waiting for it. The staff didn't rush to him like one would expect if someone suddenly turned violently ill. Instead, they'd exchanged a few more words, let the scene play out, and at last came to his side.

William was a predator and knew predatory behavior when he spotted it. He'd lulled his victims into believing he was there to help, much like he was doing now with the woman. She was distraught and in need of a knight in shining armor. William was more than happy to play the role.

"What's your name again?" he asked over his shoulder. He planned on taking her to his cabin and wanted to use small talk to keep her defenses down. The more he was able to keep her mind distracted, the longer it would take before her internal alarm started ringing.

"Huh? Oh, it's Emily," she said. He had no clue if that was her real name or not, though it didn't matter. Slaughtered lambs didn't need a name.

"Emily? That's a pretty name." He hated this part of the game. It would be so fucking easy if they'd just follow his lead without any reservations, but that was never the case unless they were drunk or high and Emily didn't seem to be either. When he was younger, he used to enjoy this part of the game, the hunt. Now, it was all about the kill.

"Thanks. It was my grandma's name."

William grunted, not giving a damn. It could have been a dead dog's name that her parents decided to reuse for all he cared. All he wanted was to slice her flesh and carve her meat from the bone.

He paused. Through the windows on the doors, he could see the man he'd met before, called himself Sam. Clearly, it was a fake name. Everyone went by fake names on the Coastal Express. William smiled. Sam would meet his blade, too. He was sure of it. Was "Sam" hunting for him? He'd placed a call to law enforcement before embarking on the trip, taunting the alphabet boys. William wasn't stupid. He knew they were out to get him, and he admired men like the Zodiac, who taunted the boys in blue while still managing to have his fun. That was why he'd done it. Not only would he taunt them, but he'd slay them, too. Proving to everyone paying attention that the Rail Car Cleaver was the baddest of all serial killers.

And if "Sam" wasn't one of the boys in blue? Well, that was fine too. One more body for the final tally. If there was an undercover here, acting on his anonymous tip, that would make things more interesting, and if not, then things would be much easier.

But it wasn't time to deal with Sam yet, so he improvised. "Let's try the other side of the train," William said. "I think the infirmary might be back there." He nodded in the opposite direction of where they were headed, glancing quickly to see Sam moving further away as though he were crossing to the next car.

The staff didn't pay much attention to them. And why would they? With everything going on aboard, the Coastal Express knew discretion and secrecy were of the utmost importance. William thought he had a good idea of what might happen to those who *didn't* understand the importance of those virtues. And money, of course. He knew the staff must be paid handsomely to forget about the things they witnessed and covered up on the Coastal Express. In the end, money trumps everything.

When William had slaughtered the couple earlier, he remembered going to the dining car afterwards and sipping on a brandy, trying to calm his nerves. Every time a member of the staff had walked by, his anxiety increased, but each time they passed him by, they never so much as gave him a second look. Eventually he'd returned to the scene of the crime, wanting to admire his handywork, but to his surprise it had been thoroughly cleaned. If he didn't know any better, he'd have thought he was in the wrong room, or hallucinating.

It wasn't too long after that an envelope was slipped under the door, notifying him of a large sum of money that he was being charged for *clean-up*. He was confused for a moment, until he realized the implications, and what he was actually being charged for. From that point on, he could think of nothing else but all the fun he could have. The only ceiling to his fun was money. And his father had plenty of it to burn. It was simply up to him to figure out how to gain access to the money that was squirreled away in various accounts and investments. It would take time, but he would be able to get the money necessary to make the next trip one for the ages.

Soon, Emily would be part of the history he was writing in real time.

Emily stayed close behind him, following like a good puppy. Like most puppies he'd met in life, this one would die, too. The weight of the cleaver in his jacket made him smile. *Come on, little puppy. Come to daddy*, he thought. She was making this too easy. He couldn't wait to see the look in her eyes when she realized what he was really doing. Just like the puppies, the *Emily's* of the world never understood what was in store for them until it was too late. But unlike them, at least in her case, she'd know what was happening, and that made his cock tingle in his pants.

CHAPTER 12

Emily followed William, backtracking through the train until they'd gone past the dining car and more sleeper cars. The car they found themselves in now was different than the ones she'd seen earlier. She wasn't sure if William knew where he was going. She followed him out of necessity, not implicit trust. What other choice did she have? She should have paid better attention following the men who'd whisked Kurt away, but between the slight buzz from the alcohol, the speed at which his illness attacked, and the sheer absurdness of the scene — not to mention the staff's refusal to give her answers — she'd simply not paid attention to her surroundings. The car they were in now had a center aisle and on either side were metal doors with two deadbolts each. A sterile scent replaced the smells of breakfast and offered hope that they were closer to the infirmary.

"What is this car?" Emily asked. William turned back and smiled.

"Truthfully, I don't know. The staff are excellent when it comes to food and drink service, but it seems nobody around here likes to answer questions. These look like freezer doors to me. Maybe it's where they keep the food."

"But why double lock them? It seems like overkill to me."

William grunted, shrugged his shoulders.

Emily tried the handle of another door at random while passing through, finding it locked, too.

When they reached the end of the car, William opened the door and they crossed to the next one.

This one was another sleeper car like the previous ones on the other side of the dining car. Emily didn't understand why they weren't all linked together. It seemed to her like that would have been the obvious design decision.

William nodded for her to follow, and she was starting to get the sense that maybe he wasn't really trying to help her. It's not that he said or did anything wrong, but truth be told, Emily didn't trust men much to begin with, and she thought most women would probably agree. Hopefully, William would turn out to be nothing more than a good Samaritan.

He began to speak when the door ahead of them opened and a staff member walked through. It was a man, middle-aged, and with short brown hair and a curly q mustache.

"Hey, what are ya doing in here?" he said with a distinctly British accent. "This is staff quarters. Turn around now and head back to the dining car."

William cocked his head slightly. "Staff?" he asked.

"This car is off limits. Please, if you don't mind," he said, waving his hand toward the rear door of the car. "I don't want to call security."

Emily was more than happy to turn back. The more time she spent with William, the worse she felt about the vibes she was getting.

Now in the lead, Emily exited the car, passed through the storage car, and back into the dining car. Roxy noticed her and waved excitedly.

"Hey Sugar, come on and have some dinner with me." She had changed and was in a new, clean set of clothes and sat at a small table by herself.

William grabbed her arm, his strong fingers digging into her arm.

"We can keep looking for the infirmary. I think I know where to find it," he said. Emily shrugged out of his grip and turned to face him.

"I appreciate your help, William, but I think I might stay here with my friend, Roxy."

At the rejection, an almost imperceptible change crept over his features before returning to normal. Had Emily not been on high alert, she might not have even noticed, but it caused her to shiver. Whatever his intentions, it was clear they weren't for the best, and Emily was thankful she'd developed a strong distrust of the opposite sex. She noticed his hand slide across his sportscoat before he quickly pulled it away.

"Come on, darlin'" Roxy said, "sit your pretty little ass down and have a bite to eat."

"How can I deny that?" Emily said to William. "Thank you for trying to help. Maybe we'll run into each other later." *I fucking hope not*, she added in her head.

"Good fucking luck finding your man," William said. "I'll be around." He stormed off, leaving the dining car.

As she watched him leave, a waiter stopped by with a glass of water and asked Emily if she'd like something else to drink. She absently replied she'd like a vodka martini and he left to get it.

"Hun, you gotta be careful who you associate with here on this train. That man ain't got the slightest good intentions about himself," Roxy said, her southern drawl soothing to Emily's ears. Emily's thoughts were brought back to the moment, and she smiled warmly at Roxy.

"Thank you for helping. He was starting to give me bad vibes, you know?"

Roxy reached her hand across the table and gently placed it on Emily's. "I've got your back. Don't you go worrying about that man."

Emily enjoyed the warm touch. It felt like when Kurt used to hold her hand when they were out in public. He didn't do that anymore. It was such a simple gesture, but one that conveyed so much feeling. It was odd to her to experience that from a strange woman she barely knew.

"Why are you helping me?" Emily blurted out. She breathed in deeply, shocked by her own forwardness, but it was the truth. Why had Roxy wanted to do anything for her? For all she knew, Roxy could be dangerous.

"You remind me a lot of myself. Lost, heart-broken, unsure of herself. Sound about right?"

Emily couldn't deny it. Since Kurt's infidelity, she'd felt all those things and more. She let out a heavy sigh. "Yeah. It's been a rough few years."

Roxy nodded and took her hand off Emily's. Almost immediately Emily longed for her touch, the loss of it reminded her of someone yanking a throw blanket off you on a chilly evening.

"I think I might have something to ease your mind," Roxy said. Emily waited for her to suggest a drug of some kind. She hadn't used anything harder than marijuana, even in the beginning stages of their relationship when Kurt had pressured her into dropping acid.

"I'm not into drugs. I'll drink, but that's as far as I'll go," Emily said in anticipation of Roxy's question. The waiter had returned with her drink and asked them both if they were ready to order.

"I'll have oysters with asparagus and a dinner salad. Give me the house vinaigrette with that, please," Roxy said.

"Do you have any soup?" Emily asked. It was a boring choice, but it was her go-to comfort food and helped settle her stomach when she was anxious.

"We've got clam chowder or a broccoli cheese soup, ma'am," the waiter replied.

"I'll have the clam chowder."

"Very well," the waiter said, then turned and left them alone.

"Drugs? Honey, I ain't about no drugs," Roxy said. Her lips curled up in a lurid smile. "I'm talking about something far more enjoyable."

Emily raised her water to her lips, trying to hide her embarrassment. How could she be so stupid? When she first met Roxy, the woman exuded sexuality and lust. The woman was absolutely trying to push something at her, but it certainly wasn't a drug.

"Oh," Emily said, her response muffled by the glass she still held at her lips.

"I fully anticipate your man will be back in your cabin soon enough. Until he does, maybe you and I could entertain each other. What do ya think, sugar?" Emily saw the desire in Roxy's eyes. It reminded her of the way Kurt looked at her when he had a raging hard-on and was trying to see if he could con her into sex before giving up and opting to masturbate.

Emily's face grew redder. She put the glass down. There was no way she could hide behind it all night. She'd never done anything other than kiss a woman before. Kurt had tried getting her to bring another woman in the bed, but she had shot down the idea as soon as he'd expressed it. It had intrigued her, and she might have entertained it if she wasn't so sure watching Kurt fuck another woman would send her spiraling. And that was before he'd cheated. Had he broached the subject again, she'd probably kill him.

"How about we have some dinner first and then go from there?" Emily replied. She needed to kill time to make sure William wasn't lurking around but was still worried about Kurt's whereabouts.

"That's not a bad idea. You're gonna need some fuel," Roxy said.

The conversation turned to mundane things like favorite color and music and other nonsense things that Emily was sure that Roxy was lying about. There was no way Roxy was a New Kids on the Block fan. But still, their conversation did settle Emily's nerves. The chowder helped, too.

When they were done and the dishes were cleared from the table, Emily had relaxed enough that she wasn't as concerned about Kurt's return as she was earlier. Roxy had her convinced that while, yes, she didn't know *where* the infirmary was, that didn't mean something was going on. They had medical staff on hand to assist with whatever the passengers needed. The train was mysterious by nature, and they might not want people poking around the areas meant for staff. There were a lot of passengers on board. If anything, they were probably too busy taking care of Kurt, and anyone else on board who might be sick or injured, to reach out to Emily and calm her nerves. And if he had something like the flu, well, at that point, they might want to keep him quarantined for the health and safety of the rest of the passengers.

The conversation took a turn back toward the interesting side of things. It seemed Roxy couldn't keep her desire to herself. "Wanna stop by my room?" Roxy asked. The anticipation in her eyes brought a nervous energy to Emily. She was conflicted. The prospect of trying something new with a beautiful woman like Roxy was mixed with the guilt of cheating on Kurt. But was it really cheating? It was more like experimenting, a dalliance with a fantasy Kurt had always tried to manifest. And if it was cheating, did she care? He'd already cheated on her. At worst, she was repaying the favor. Maybe that would help them put everything behind them and start fresh.

"Yeah," Emily said. "Let's have some fun." She covered her mouth with her hand, surprised that she had spoken the words out loud.

Roxy smiled. "Then let's get ta moving, sugar. Ain't no time to waste."

Colton exited the room, letting the door close behind him. His face was flushed, his entire body felt warm, despite the climate-controlled temperature of the train. He could feel the sweat dripping down the small of his back. He felt a static creeping up from the base of his skull, enveloping his entire head. It usually started off small as background noise, but Colton knew if he didn't force it away, it would grow louder. He'd been able to quell it with alcohol earlier, but it was back, and he knew if he didn't figure out a way to compartmentalize it soon, he'd be in full on panic attack mode. This latest onset had been triggered by the woman's body. As soon as he left the room, it came back.

When it came to female victims, it always did. Whenever an especially heinous crime was enacted on a woman, it made him think of his Jessica. Made him wonder if she had met a similar fate. He knew it was likely. She'd been missing too long. Everyone knew the stats on missing children. After a few days, the odds of finding the child alive were unlikely. For that reason, a part of Colton was glad they'd never found her. He didn't need closure. He knew she was dead. At least if they never recovered her body, he couldn't be forced to confront whatever hell she'd endured before her eventual murder. No body meant no evidence. No evidence meant on those nights when his mind wandered, he could lie to himself. Tell himself she'd gone peacefully and had not been made to suffer before her brutal demise.

Maybe the killer was the Cleaver. Maybe it was some other monster. Either way, it was Colton's responsibility to put an end to it. For the Marshals, for anyone who had a loved one brutalized by some psychopath. And more importantly, for Jessica.

With that in mind, he worked his way through the cars, taking a mental note of every person he passed, his brain now working like a computer. He was firing on all cylinders in the zone, so to speak. With the alcohol having faded from his system, it was easier to focus, and he was able to use the laser focus to keep the static at bay, rather than the booze. How long he could manage without the booze? That was another story. He was an addict, and he'd need his fix again at some point.

He hadn't seen the man in some time and had no clue where he'd gone off to. It was his only lead; he needed to find the son of a bitch.

Perhaps the man had found another victim. He passed through the bar quickly, glad the woman he'd been speaking with was gone. There was no time for distractions right now, certainly not pleasures of the flesh. And how he'd been tempted. The word 'succubus' came to mind when he thought of her. Not that he believed in such things, but the way she'd been able to *almost* get him to cave in, like she had a power over men. Or maybe Colton was nothing more than a lonely man. It had been ages since he'd been with a woman. Burying yourself in work, alcohol, and grief didn't leave much time for anything else.

If his search for the suspect left him empty-handed, he'd do his best to avoid her for the duration of their travels. It made more sense to question other passengers rather than put himself in a compromised position once more. And she didn't seem to know much more than him, either.

Someone had to know who this guy was, or where he was. And if he turned out to be a dead end, it would be beneficial to have gotten to speak with more of the passengers.

COLTON CAME AWAY from the search empty handed. It had been a fruitless endeavor. He'd returned to his room and passed out, sleeping with a pair of noise-reducing earmuffs to drown out the sound of the man he'd left tied up in the bathroom. He'd have to do something about that soon. He was going to have to use the shower at some point. The train did have scattered public toilets he could use to do his business, but how the hell was he supposed to blend in and complete the mission if he went the whole trip without taking a shower?

Maybe I can use Arianna's shower?

God, he needed to get that woman out of his head, but it was tough when the last image burned into his mind had been her sucking her own wetness off her finger. Thinking of it made his morning wood feel as if it were about to explode.

He brewed a pot of coffee and ran through his notes,

making sure he hadn't missed anything. Waking up from the nap after going as long as he had without another drink made it tough to focus, his temples throbbing. Hopefully, the coffee would ease the pressure on his skull because he really needed to get this case taken care of ASAP. So far, it was only one body, but who knew how many there were lying around the train, or how many more there would be if he didn't find this guy? It was a train, for Christ's sake. Where the fuck could he possibly be?

Colton resolved to end this tonight. No more thinking about circling to square one if he couldn't find the man he was looking for. An attitude like that bred failure. He *would* find the man. He *would* crack the case. He *would* stop whatever evil was happening on this train. And when that was done? He'd stop the pieces of shit running this operation. A sex train was one thing, but if the shit he'd heard from the other passengers was true, which he now believed it was, he didn't care if it was the last thing he did. He'd make a file on this train and work on it every single day until he died, if that was what it took.

Colton chugged his coffee and placed the mug down, leaving the rest of the coffee on the burner as he went to see this thing through.

CHAPTER 14

Arianna woke in bed next to the elder gentleman she'd selected. The bed, saturated in blood, squelched as she sat up. She'd wanted that man who'd called himself Sam, even had him in her grasp, but he had gotten distracted and took off. The geezer had been no fun. Old men were too easy. She craved a new experience. Too busy trapping old men like the black widow she was, she'd never fucked a man south of fifty before. Every man she'd ever been with had been so old, each erection threatened a heart attack.

Speaking of dick, she thought, twirling around his severed member. It had been pretty big, and Arianna had had her fun with it before torturing and killing the man. He must have been a stud in his younger days, with a piece like that. Thinking about how she'd stuffed his severed cock down his throat to choke him with it had turned her on, and she absent-mindedly played with her pussy. The desire between her legs grew to be too much, and before she'd be able to get on with her day, she'd need to take care of herself.

Arianna rolled the soft, severed cock around in the blood

before placing it against her labia. Luckily for her, the old man had been a shower, not a grower, and so the severed pecker was still serviceable as a fuck toy, once she'd managed to push it past her glistening lips.

She thrusted herself with the cock until she came, riding the euphoric waves until they washed the desire away, leaving a mental clarity that would allow her to continue her day, and figure out a plan for later.

She showered herself off, washing away the blood. The deed had been done in the man's room. That hadn't been planned, though it worked out to her benefit. At least this way she wouldn't need to worry about a body. Maybe they'd hunt her down later, but with some luck, maybe she'd get away with the murder.

After she'd dried herself off, she put last night's outfit back on and drank a glass of water. Though the soundproofing kept the roar of the train's movement at bay, she felt the vibration of the tracks below her feet. Her mind was blank as she focused on the feel of the tracks below her until an idea struck her out of the blue. If she couldn't ensnare the man who had called himself Sam in her little game, maybe she'd try for a different target.

Maybe it would be fun to give it a go with one of the staff members. One of those burly guys that had shown people to their rooms. It didn't matter how big a man was. When their dicks were leading the way, self-defense was not something they'd be thinking of.

She smiled and made her way back to her room. Maybe her bed would see some of the action tonight.

CHAPTER 15

Nervous energy surged through Emily as she entered Roxy's cabin. Was she really going to go through with this? How was it any different from Kurt banging that girl? It wasn't. That's the point.

"Hey, hun, are you ok?" Roxy asked. Her sultry southern accent melted Emily's thoughts until they smoldered in her head.

"Oh, yeah, I'm fine."

Roxy raised an eyebrow and offered a questioning look. Emily slipped past her and took a seat on the couch, turning her head to watch the scenery go by.

It was funny. All this time spent on the train and she barely looked outside. A whole new view of the country flashed past her, and she kept looking inward. What had she missed by focusing on Kurt? The vast wilderness of the country was something she had never really contemplated before. *What mysteries are out there?* she wondered.

"Here, maybe this will help ease your mind," Roxy said, handing Emily a drink.

"Thanks," she said, taking the drink with no expectation of actually consuming it. She got the sense that if she rejected it that Roxy might take offense.

Roxy sat in a plush chair to Emily's right and turned her gaze out the window as well. The pair of them watched lush pine forests race by the window. Valleys were covered in varying shades of greens and browns, a blur of color. Sunlight streamed through the thin clouds, bringing with it life and hope. In the distance, a river snaked through the valley and around a bend where it disappeared. A small town stretched across the horizon. Emily wondered if anyone in the town had a clue as to the true nature of the train that they saw crossing their view. She imagined they'd probably be more than a little surprised.

"Sugar, you don't need to worry about a thing," Roxy said. "We can take it as slow as you want."

Emily felt her cheeks blush. Coming with Roxy to her cabin was her decision, and she knew what she was signing up for, but part of her still felt guilty for what she was thinking about doing.

Emily turned to Roxy, the drink still in her hand. "I appreciate that," she said. "I've, well, never been with a woman before. This is all new to me."

Roxy smiled and for a moment, Emily felt like prey just before the predator strikes. But within Roxy's lovely smile was a certain comfort that Emily couldn't resist. A snake charmer with nothing more than soft, ruby red lips.

Roxy took Emily's glass from her and set it on the table. Her heart thumped in her chest. Excitement raced through her body, filling her with such a sexual charge that she was surprised by its power.

Roxy got on her knees in front of her. Emily's breathing grew rapid.

"Let's set a boundary," Roxy said. "If we go too far and you want to stop, we will use a safe word. If you need to stop or get to a point where it's too much, you just say 'Bluebird' and we'll go to a full stop, no questions asked. What's the safe word again?"

Emily couldn't think, she could barely breathe. It took a moment, but she finally replied, "Bluebird."

"That's it. Say the word if you need to."

Emily nodded. Roxy reached out and grasped her hand, stroking it gently. "Lean back, darlin.' We'll take it slow before moving on."

With a mixture of unbridled excitement and a nervous hesitation, Emily obeyed Roxy's request. She leaned back against the couch while Roxy slowly parted her legs. She hadn't shaved this morning and instinctively tried to close her legs. Roxy's firm grip wouldn't allow it. Should she use the safe word?

Roxy slid her fingers under the waistband of Emily's pants and slowly pulled them down, exposing her nakedness. Emily was thrilled and anxious, a bundle of nerves all set to explode at the slightest touch.

"A most beautiful pair of lips," Roxy purred. She pushed her hair out of her face and leaned closer until Emily felt her breath over her vagina. She squeezed her legs, but Roxy wasn't having it and instead forced them open even wider. Emily felt completely exposed. She knew this was going to be a different kind of experience, but now about ready to jump in full steam, she worried that maybe it was the wrong thing to do. How would she feel if Kurt did that to her? She'd already experienced the pain of infidelity. Could she do that to him?

Before she could blurt out the word 'Bluebird,' Roxy pulled her open with her fingers and began teasing her clit with her tongue. Usually, Emily needed to be warmed up before jumping into oral like that, but the walk to Roxy's cabin, and the leadup to this moment, had already gotten her motor going. There was something alluring about Roxy, something so subtle she couldn't put her finger on it, but the woman had her ready to melt before her pants had even come off. And wow, did she know what she was doing with that tongue. Each delicate stroke sent tiny shocks of excitement through Emily's body. Roxy's fingers explored inside of her, filling her and spreading her open even wider. She felt Roxy's index and middle finger move in a come-hither motion, rubbing her g-spot. Roxy's tongue continued to flick across her clit, soft and yet powerful. Emily closed her eyes and let the woman do her magic.

She moaned and placed her hand on Roxy's head, gently cradling her. Roxy applied more pressure with her two fingers, and Emily was getting ready to explode.

Roxy continued for several minutes, Emily's moans getting louder as she approached climax before Roxy backed off, edging her.

Roxy looked up at her, her chin and lips soaked in Emily's juices. "Hun, you doin' alright?" she asked. Emily could only nod. Her heart was racing, and her excitement had built up so much that she wanted nothing more than to orgasm.

"Ready to take it up a notch?"

Emily nodded. Roxy stood in front of her and, for a

moment, Emily felt a loss, as though she'd offended the woman and wouldn't get a chance to experience the rest. But after Roxy came back from plucking something out of her bag and kneeling in front of her again, she settled down.

Roxy had brought lube and squirted it all over her hand, rubbing it on like lotion. "You remember the word, right?" Emily nodded vigorously. *What was she about to do?* she wondered.

Roxy spread Emily's legs wider and with her lubed hand, inserted two fingers. She worked them around for a bit and then squeezed another digit, stretching Emily open further. Roxy continued fucking Emily like that, and when Emily's body began to tense, Roxy stuck a fourth finger in her. Her groans were now fevered, animalistic. The feeling of being stretched was completely new to her. Kurt wasn't small, but he wasn't big either. This was something entirely different.

But Roxy wasn't done with Emily yet. She balled her hand into a fist and instantly sent shockwaves through Emily. The sensation was a combination of pain and ecstasy. She could feel every little ridge on Roxy's fist, every knuckle and finger joint. She glanced down and only saw Roxy's wrist; the rest was engulfed in her well-lubricated pussy.

"My, my. You are an eager one," Roxy said. She slowly moved her fist inside of Emily, filling her entirely. Her eyes fluttered at the twin sensation of pain and pleasure. She'd heard of fisting before and had even seen it a couple of times in some old porn VHS tapes that Kurt rented, but feeling it was something else.

She spread her legs wider, allowing Roxy greater access to her already stretched pussy. She wanted more; she wanted all of her. Grasping Roxy's wrist, she moved it like a dildo to pleasure herself. Roxy purred and pinched her own nipples as Emily moaned louder with each thrust of Roxy's fist.

Her oncoming orgasm was almost here, and she clung to the growing pleasure, focusing on it and allowing the pain to accentuate it. She groaned louder and Roxy thrust her fist faster inside of her.

"Oh fuck, yes!" Emily said.

Roxy thrust faster, her movements so quick that Emily barely registered what was going on now. She was fully focused on the orgasm. Her eyes rolled to the back of her head, the lids fluttering. The orgasm vibrated her entire body. Her legs shook, her abdominal muscles tensed. She clung to Roxy's fist with her vagina, grappling it in a powerful, clenching motion as she came.

"Yes, yes, yes!" she shouted as another wave of orgasm made her body shudder. If she came any harder, she might have a heart attack.

Roxy slowly brought her fist to a stop as Emily's orgasm had reached its climax and was now starting to wane. Emily breathed heavily, sweat trickled down her forehead.

When Roxy pulled her fist free, she felt empty and abandoned, wishing she had left it inside of her and filling her.

"That was fucking amazing," Emily breathed. Roxy smiled at her, then glanced down at her spread open legs.

"Oh dear," she said, "It may have been too much." She felt Roxy's finger trace the inside of her labia before raising it in front of her, red with blood. Roxy smiled, then licked it clean, closing her eyes and savoring it.

Alarms blared in Emily's head. Did she just…taste her blood? What the fuck was wrong with her?

Roxy leaned close and gently pushed Emily's matted hair from her forehead. "That was just the beginning," she said, planting a kiss on her forehead. She offered a wink, and Emily tried not to let what Roxy did with her blood ruin what Roxy had just done to her.

CHAPTER 16

Hours had passed, and Colton was still no closer to finding his mark. How could this man elude him so effortlessly? Did he know who Colton was? Did he have an in at the task force? Had Colton blown his own cover? He didn't think either of those were the case, but he couldn't deny that of the two scenarios, the latter was certainly plausible.

Colton sat at a table, eating dinner alone. He hated eating dinner like nothing was going on, but he didn't have much of a choice either. This was an extended undercover mission, and he was alone. Getting to the bottom of things could take time, regardless of his self-promise to resolve everything tonight. Things rarely pan out the way you hope them to, and Colton couldn't just forgo the quieter parts of the mission simply because he felt like he should be doing something else.

The filet mignon was delicious, cooked rare. The meat practically melted in his mouth, its juices perfectly mingling with the char on the outside of the steak. He tried to remember this was part of the mission, too. His eyes remained on a swivel as he swallowed the tender meat, washing it down with a sip of cola. He had just one glass of wine while waiting for his meal. Colton told himself it was so he wouldn't go through a withdrawal during the mission. He knew that was bullshit, but at least he'd only had the one drink. He hadn't lost complete control yet.

The mashed potatoes were just as good. He'd never tasted potatoes quite like these. It was a shame, what the rumors were behind the scenes, because Colton could see this train being a big hit as a luxury vacation, like cruising on the land for the uber rich. How many of the people riding right now were innocent? There had to be some normal rich folk here. He couldn't imagine every person here was involved in shady dealings.

Or maybe they were. The food turned in his stomach as he thought about all the human scum that might partake in something like this. He could see it all clearly. The worst of the worst. Drug kingpins, high-ranking cartel members, human traffickers, the shadowy elites of the world. The ruling class that had everyone under their thumbs behind the scenes. Colton had no doubt they existed. There were rumors of such a class going back hundreds of years. The notion was often dismissed as nothing more than conspiracy, but the way the world operated, Colton didn't necessarily believe it to be true, but he also wouldn't be surprised to discover it *was* true.

From the corner of his eye, Colton saw his only suspect whisk through the dining car. He tossed his fork aside, pushed his chair out, and followed.

The man walked quickly, his long legs propelling him forward as he dragged a woman who'd clearly had too much to drink along for the ride.

Colton increased his pace, closing the distance as quickly

as he could. He heard the woman giggle as she spouted out what Colton believed to be a room number.

So, he isn't taking her back to his room.

They went to the next car, one of the sleeper cars. Colton closed the gap further and shouted at the pair. "Hey, miss, are you ok?" He knew it was risky, knew he could be breaking his cover. Whether it was the instinct to save a life, or just one more bad decision at work, Colton didn't know, but his gut told him he needed to intervene.

The bald man and the woman both turned. "We're about to be a lot more than ok, mister," she responded. The man smiled, nodding.

Colton tried again. "Miss, are you with that man?" He ran through all the scenarios of what to do next. None of them were great.

She slurred her words. "Right now I'm with him, but if you leave us alone, I'm about to be *on top* of him."

"He's a goddamn killer, that's what he is!" Colton yelled, choosing the one option that he knew was the riskiest. If the man really was the Rail Car Cleaver, he had to do something to protect the woman. If he wasn't, well, then he'd just blown his cover and this would probably be the end of his tenure. He'd be forced to take a desk job, maybe even retire, the shame of botching the biggest mission of his career, staining his memory forever. They kept walking, and Colton picked up the pace to catch up.

"Sure is a killer, because he's about to slay this pussy," the woman yelled back, laughing like it was the funniest thing she'd ever said.

The bald man, addressing Colton, spoke. "Sam, that's what you said your name was, right?" he said, winking. "My earlier invite was just that, an earlier invite. I'm afraid you aren't invited to this party, especially after an insult like that. However, if you feel compelled to party with me, we can arrange something at a future time." The bald man nodded at the passing security staff. "Gentleman, this man intends on interrupting my party. Please make sure that he is seen to his room, and away from my friend's."

The two large gentlemen, whose button-down vests appeared to be bursting from massive chest muscles, the arms of the undershirts filled with all they could handle, stepped between Colton and the man and woman.

"Sir, please turn around and remove yourself from the area," said the large man with a 70s porn mustache.

Colton shook his head. "You don't understand," he said, "that man means to harm that woman."

The other large man spoke. "Sir, that woman is with him of her own accord. She looks consenting enough to me. The first time we ask you. The second time, we tell you. So how do you wanna play this?"

"Oh, fuck this," Colton said as he launched a straight right-handed punch that connected with the man's nose, shattering it. Blood spurted from the ruined nose and the man grabbed his face.

"Fuck!" the man yelled as he stumbled backward.

His partner was quick, quicker than Colton, and the moment Colton had launched the punch, he was already lunging, spearing his body into Colton even as his partner screamed in pain. The man's large frame collided with Colton's ribs, throwing him into the wall.

Colton grunted from the impacts of both the man, and the wall, and though he wasn't quick enough to prevent the man from spearing him, he recovered quickly, planting his legs, preventing the man from bringing him to the ground. He turned, keeping his back to the wall as he wrapped his arms around the man's waist from above, pushing his full body-weight down on the man. Quickly, he alternated sharp elbows to the man's kidneys. The elbow's landed precisely where Colton intended, and the man dropped to the ground like a sack of potatoes. Colton followed up with a kick to the man's face, sending his consciousness to the void.

Colton did a quick visual sweep of the area. His suspect and the drunk woman were gone. He stepped over the two goons and began pounding on the doors in the area, unsure which one they had disappeared into. The soundproofing of the rooms made it impossible to hear what was going on behind closed doors.

While he was pounding on one of the doors, screaming for the occupant to open up, Colton was unaware of the goon whose nose he had shattered approaching him with a stun gun in his hand.

He heard a crackle and then lost control of his body as the man kept the stun gun against his body for far longer than the manufacturer's suggested use.

Colton twitched on the ground. The man grabbed him under his arms and began to drag him across the floor, blood pouring from his shattered nose, his unconscious buddy still crumpled on the floor. The passengers in the area dispersed from the scene, not wanting to be further involved.

CHAPTER 17

Cleaned up and ready for more fun, Arianna made her way straight to the bar. Hair down, tight dress, pumps. If looks could kill, she wouldn't be on the prowl looking to do the deed herself. Which was fine, in her opinion. She'd killed before she'd ever stepped foot on the Coastal Express, but she hadn't realized how much she'd liked it until now. Was it her abusers who made her this way? Or was it always there, deep down? Locked in a cage within her, and the men who'd wronged her had simply been the jailers holding the key.

She didn't care. Arianna wasn't a psychologist. All she knew is she wanted to keep doing it. And she would, for as long as she could get away with it. She thought back to her most recent man, thought of fucking herself with the severed cock, and she felt the heat growing between her legs, spreading throughout her body. She had no idea what had come over her. She'd never been squeamish, but she'd also never been one to practice necrophilia, either.

For her next bit of fun, she wanted to find a real man, not some old geezer trying to relive his glory days. This time she was dead set on finding a man who could screw her brains out. And after she made her target come, when he was experiencing his post-orgasm euphoria and his nut was still dripping out of her pussy, she'd swoop in for the kill.

Men were simple. Even the biggest, toughest, most macho men reverted to little more than defenseless children moments after shooting a load. Arianna had always known the key to getting what you want from a man was asking him right before he came. She thought the key to overpowering one was striking moments after.

The bar was packed, couples and throuples and individuals seemed to be on the prowl. Drink in hand, Arianna prowled the bar in search of prey. During her sweep of the place, she locked eyes with a large man dressed like the service staff. Clearly, he was the muscle around here. He spoke to another similarly dressed man standing next to him. She circled closer, straining to hear their conversation. She couldn't tell what they were saying but thought one of them had mouthed something about a disturbance. Were they talking about her? She didn't think so. How would anyone know? Arianna didn't recall seeing any cameras, and if privacy and secrecy were part of the experience, then it wouldn't make sense to have them around.

The large man she'd locked eyes with kept his gaze on her as she approached. His partner shook his head and walked off, clearly disagreeing with something he'd said.

This is the one, she thought. He fit the bill perfectly for what she'd intended. Rough sex and a bloody death. She felt powerful just thinking about how she'd drain the life from him at his most vulnerable moment, snuff him out like nothing more than a matchstick. For a moment, she wondered what if she couldn't overpower him? What if she failed? The thought went as quickly as it came, Arianna realizing she didn't much care what happened to her.

"Hey there," she said, taking a sip from her drink.

He nodded his head, "Ma'am."

"You look lonely over here. I thought maybe you'd like some company."

"I appreciate that, miss, but I'm not lonely. I'm working."

"Oh, I don't know," she said, reaching for his crotch and running her palm up the front of his pants, "you seem like someone who might like some company."

"Mmm. Now *that,* you're right about. But I've gotta finish my shift."

"Where's the fun in that?"

"If it's all the same to you, I'd rather not lose my job."

Arianna stepped closer, whispering in his ear, "It's not as fun when there's no danger."

She felt his bulge against her leg. Men were all the same. They might act like they didn't want it but push the issue enough and the head between the legs eventually takes control of the one between the shoulders.

He cleared his throat. "Come with me, but we've gotta make it look good. Play along," he said as he grabbed her arm and spun her around, wrenching it behind her back.

"Ah, what the hell!"

"Yeah, that's a good girl."

Arianna walked as he roughly guided her by the arm. She didn't have to try too hard to play along with his game. Her arm felt like it was going to rip out of its socket at any moment. That was fine by her. She'd pay him back soon enough.

He opened the door and pushed her inside, kicking it closed behind him. Arianna didn't mind the rough stuff. In fact, she preferred it, but she'd certainly keep the pain in mind when she took her turn dishing revenge out.

"It's dark in here," she purred, slipping out of her dress.

"We have to be discreet," the man replied. "You don't understand anything about my bosses. It won't be good for either of us if someone finds us here."

She'd suspected the people in charge of this operation were up to no good but hearing it from a man as imposing as the gentleman she'd caught in her web still sent a chill down her spine. If he was afraid of the repercussions, what might they do to her?

She stepped closer, her eyes adjusting to the dark, though it was tough to see everything in the room. She could make out a table in the corner, and two massive cylinder-shaped objects on either side of what she assumed to be some sort of control panel, but in the dark she really couldn't be sure.

"Where are we?" she asked.

"Depends on who you ask," he said. Arianna heard his belt sliding off his pants and the clatter of the buckle hitting the floor. "In case of an emergency, it can be used as a sick bay. Problem is, for whatever reason, when sick passengers come in here, they don't usually leave."

Arianna had no idea what he was talking about, and before she could ask, he pressed up against her and they embraced. She felt his hand slide up her thigh and across her wet sex. When his finger reached her hood and lightly grazed her clit, she shivered. Their tongues danced together, and she reached down and stroked his shaft. It wasn't as big as she'd hoped, but it was big enough to get the job done.

He grunted and turned her around, pushing her to the other end of the room. Her thighs bumped against the panel at the other side, and he bent her over it. The man kicked her feet apart and licked his hand before running it along her pussy, not that she needed the help getting wet. She hated being bossed around throughout her daily life, but when it came to sex, she liked a man who would dominate her. She moaned at his touch, anticipating what would come next, and she gasped as his erect cock plunged inside of her tight hole.

They rutted like that, quick, powerful thrusts from behind until they both came, Arianna's orgasm causing her to cry out as she felt his semen squirt inside her.

Neither of them had noticed when Arianna's hand hit the button on the control panel, disengaging locks on the large cylinders. The sound of their animalistic mating had over-powered the whirring and hissing. But in the moments after they finished, and the doors slid open, they heard a liquid rushing out, splashing the ground. A revolting smell, a mixture of rotting meat and blood, flooded the room.

"What the hell is that?" Arianna said.

"I don't know. What the hell did you do?" The man was already stepping back into his pants.

"God, that fucking stinks," she said as the warm liquid pooled around her feet. She cried out in disgust and took a few quick steps back. Her foot slipped on the slick floor, and she fell backward on her ass. Arianna scrambled to her feet, her palms sticky with the fluid.

She heard a hissing noise in the darkness, this one not

mechanical, and before she could react, something crashed into her chest, slicing at her bare skin.

She screamed, her heart pounding and her skin on fire. She was confused and scared to death. A massive weight pressed down upon her and from the angle she was at, she couldn't tell what was attacking her. But it was strong, easily holding her down as it rendered her flesh.

The thing's head shot forward with blistering speed, and she felt an immense pressure clamp down on her neck moments before it pulled back, its razor teeth ripping a chunk from her neck. A geyser of blood exploded from the ragged hole, painting both the thing and her fuck buddy with hot arterial splatter.

As Arianna's screams turned to gurgling noises and she was ripped to shreds by tooth and claw, the man pulled his pistol from the holster in his vest and shot at the thing. The bullet found its home in the creature's shoulder; the impact forcing its body to turn, but nothing more.

He pulled the trigger twice more and the momentary flash from the barrel revealed something straight out of a nightmare.

Another shot. In the glow, the thing reared its head up and screeched, blood spraying from another bullet wound.

He pulled the trigger, revealing a lean, muscular form with alabaster skin stretched over it.

Bang. Fangs and claws, dripping with blood.

Bang. This time the bullet hit the thing dead center in the forehead, and it fell backward, twitching on the ground while a whisp of smoke rose from the freshly created hole in its head.

The man, sweating profusely, let the expended magazine

fall to the ground and slapped a new one in the magazine well as he walked toward the thing, stopping a few inches away.

Another hiss in the dark.

The second tank. He fired two shots in the direction of the tank and turned toward the door, running for dear life.

As his hand gripped the handle, the second creature leapt at him, slamming him to the ground.

He reached behind his head, slapping at the thing as it bit into the back of his skull, ripping and tearing with long, sharp teeth and a bite like a bear trap. Flecks of skull and brain matter flew through the air as the thing feasted on the man's lifeless corpse.

CHAPTER 18

Emily didn't remember falling asleep after the fisting she received from Roxy. She didn't remember closing her eyes. She didn't remember being moved from the couch. She didn't remember being stripped naked. She didn't remember being bound by rope. But there she was. Sitting in a chair near the window as the outside world flashed by, with her hands tied together behind her back and a nasty cramp building in her shoulders and creeping up her neck.

The rhythmic motion of the train made her sway back and forth, her chest jiggling, and her hair falling in her face.

What the fuck is going on? she thought. Her mind was hazy, as though peering through frosted glass. Her wrists burned from the taut rope and when she twisted her hands to test the movement, she regretted it.

Her vagina ached. Stretched and abused by Roxy's fist, it burned, and she wanted to clean up, letting the hot water of a shower wash away the memory. She wished she'd never come back to Roxy's cabin. In the heat of the moment, she had loved the way Roxy made her feel, loved the way she made her come. But after the rush of chemicals that came with an orgasm receded, guilt was the only thing remaining.

Why had Roxy tied her up? And why couldn't she remember anything? After the workout Roxy had put her through, Emily had finally had the drink Roxy had given her, despite the shock she'd felt when seeing the woman taste her blood. She'd tried telling herself it was just some weird kink, and hoped the more she went along, the quicker she'd get to go back to her room and hopefully find Kurt.

Had the drink been drugged? Possibly. Emily sure felt like she'd been hit by a car and run over in reverse for good measure. Was this part of the "fun" Roxy had promised? Because Emily sure as fuck wasn't having a good time.

"Roxy?" she mumbled, still in a daze.

Emily struggled against the rope, but the more she moved, the more it cut into her tender wrists.

"I see you've awakened," Roxy said from behind her. Emily let out a yip. How long had Roxy been standing there watching her? Emily heard footsteps drawing closer and felt her neck hairs prickle as Roxy spoke, her warm breath tickling Emily's skin. "You taste divine. I'll enjoy draining you."

Emily's eyes widened. What the hell did that mean?

Roxy grabbed Emily's hair and yanked, the pain sharp, causing Emily to cry out.

"I've always wanted a redhead," Roxy said, a shark grin across her face. Emily felt like a bird caught in a cage, Roxy the cat outside, toying with her.

Roxy placed her hand on Emily's neck and dug her nail into her flesh. She sliced open a wound along her soft skin. Emily struggled against the bonds, but it was futile.

Roxy leaned over and latched on to the gaping wound with

her lips. Emily screamed and tried to move, but Roxy pulled her head back again, her teeth pulling the wound open further. Roxy's tongue ran the length of the wound, teasing it much like she'd done to Emily's vulva earlier.

The safe word! she thought.

"Bluebird! Bluebird! Come on, I said bluebird! You said you'd stop if I said bluebird," Emily cried out.

Roxy laughed, licked her lips. Her eyes were closed, seemingly savoring the taste of Emily's blood.

"Oops," Roxy said, placing her hand on her chin, "I lied. I know you're probably thinking 'Why am I here?' and 'What is she doing?' I know I would, if our roles were reversed." Roxy gently cradled Emily's chin, dragging her nail across the bloody gash. "Are you still glad you and Kurt went on this trip? I sure am."

"Please, just let me go. I won't tell anyone."

Roxy leaned closer and licked her open wound again, purring as she did so.

"My dear, nobody would care. And I don't think *anybody* is going to make it off the train alive this time."

Emily's eyes shot wide open. "What do you mean?"

"If I don't drain you, the sleepers will. Because I sense them, and they're not sleeping anymore. They're nasty things, abominations of my line, a sad combination of genetic mutation and scientific meddling. But they are hungry, and they need to feed. And kill. Boulder and Smith wanted me here in case things went bad, but I can't control them. They're not like me. They're something much worse."

Emily shook her head, sobbing. "I don't understand anything you're saying."

Roxy leaned forward, eye to eye with her. Emily noticed

Roxy's pupils were black, the sclera red. They hadn't looked like that before; Emily was sure of it. In that moment, she pissed herself, a warm stream that looked pink from the damage Roxy had done to her vagina.

"Oh, come now. Are you really that afraid? Have I not taken care of you? I promise you, what I'm going to do with you is nothing compared to what's in store for everyone else."

"Please, let me go! I won't tell anyone, I swear. Please, please!" Emily didn't care what Roxy claimed would happen, she just wanted to get out of the room. To find Kurt, and to get the fuck off this train.

Roxy stabbed her finger into Emily's wound, and she screamed. Roxy laughed, digging her fingers inside until Emily felt her nails scratch the bone. She howled louder, shaking back and forth.

"No!" she screamed. Fiery hot pain shot through her shoulder and down her arm.

Roxy didn't seem to care.

She grabbed Emily's skin and pulled. The tearing sound was drowned out by her screams. Blood spurted out then ran down her chest as she struggled against her restraints, her head thrashing side to side.

"Scream for me, bitch!" Roxy cackled. "Come on, get loud!"

Emily screamed. She kept fighting her restraints, flexing and thrashing about, her wrists and ankles burning from the bindings.

"You aren't going anywhere," Roxy said. "I hope you know that."

Somehow, against all odds, the bindings around Emily's wrists snapped the moment the words left Roxy's mouth. She latched on to the hope, pushed the fear out of her mind, embraced the flood of adrenaline running through her body.

Roxy, unaware the bindings were off, wriggled her finger in the wound. Emily fought through the pain and grabbed Roxy's arm.

"What the–" Roxy said, but Emily ignored the sound of her voice. She slammed Roxy's elbow against her knee. The arm broke like a twig, a sickening snap echoing through the room. A bone jutted through her skin and blood sprayed out. Roxy cried out and yanked her arm free of Emily's grip. Blood continued spurting from the wound, painting Emily's bare skin.

Roxy jumped back, and when she did, Emily went to work on the bindings on her ankles. She got one loose, but before she could get the rest, Roxy leapt at her, pressing down on her shoulder, forcing Emily's body to fold down. She hung over the back of the chair like that while Emily struggled. "Fucking bitch!" she screamed.

Emily was bleeding and out of breath, but she was so close to freeing herself and getting out of this madness. If only she could get the other woman off her.

Emily threw her weight backward, sending the two women to the floor. Emily's weight, and the chair pinned Roxy to the ground, impaling the woman's midsection with the bone from her own ruined arm. Roxy screamed in pain, and Emily used the opportunity to untie her legs. The blood running down her arm from her shoulder made it difficult for her fingers to work the knots, wasting precious time.

When her legs were finally free, she jumped up and spun around. Roxy had fallen to the floor and was trying to pull her broken arm from her midsection, screaming as it came out inch by inch. She snarled and hissed and swore, threatening Emily. Emily didn't wait. She ran from the cabin and slammed against the wall opposite the door in the hallway. Screaming for help, she ran down the hall, naked and bleeding. Behind her, she thought she heard Roxy screaming something about the sleepers.

CHAPTER 19

Vision blurry, head throbbing, Colton tried shaking away the cobwebs in his brain. One of the men pulled him by the wrists, dragging him to whatever was the destination. The lockup, Colton assumed. They had to have something to detain unruly passengers. They might not hold them for legitimate law enforcement, but it stood to reason they'd need to subdue someone, at some point, and when they did, they'd need somewhere to keep them.

My wrists.

They'd left his wrists unbound. Stupid move. They'd either assumed Colton would be unconscious far longer than he had been or were bringing him somewhere where it wouldn't matter if he was bound. Colton didn't like the possible implications of the second choice.

For now, Colton thought it best to let this idiot keep dragging him as painful as it was. The man must be expending an exorbitant amount of energy. It would be easier to make his move when the time was right.

Colton hoped the man was tiring himself out by dragging

him all that way. The effects of the stun gun had faded, and while sore, Colton felt ready for action once more.

And not a moment too soon. The man dropped his wrists and Colton opened his eyes a sliver, just enough to see and get the lay of the land.

They were in a hallway indistinguishable from any other area of the train. Aside from one feature. They'd stopped in front of a large steel door. The man swiped a keycard, and the lock disengaged with a beep. He waited while the man pushed the door open. He stopped in the middle of the doorway and shouted, "What the fuck?"

Colton saw only a glimpse of whatever the man had seen. From what Colton could tell, it wasn't good. In the room, the lights flickered on and off, giving momentary glimpses of the horrific scene between periods of thick darkness. There was blood everywhere, like a massacre had occurred. Whatever had gone down in that room, the goons hadn't had anything to do with it because the man clearly had no idea what had happened.

Now! Colton thought, scrambling to his feet. He rushed the man, tackling him from behind and using the full weight of his body to slam the man hard to the ground. He heard a sickening crack as the man's skull bore the full force of the impact. Almost immediately, blood pooled around his skull. Colton hadn't intended to kill the man, and he wasn't sure the guy was dead, but he thought it likely if he wasn't dead now, he would be soon. *Well, damn,* he thought. It would be one more thing to add to the after-action report. At this point in the mission, Colton didn't think anyone would think twice about what he did from here on out.

Colton looked up at the room the man had brought him to.

His first thought had been it was the scene of a massacre, but massacre wasn't a strong enough word to do the scene justice. The stench of blood was suffocating, and the red fluid was smeared and streaked across damn near every surface. There were at least two ruined bodies in the room, but he couldn't be sure. The state of the remains made it difficult to determine. Strips of flesh, bone, and entrails were strewn about. Biological matter was stuck to the walls, running down to the floor, leaving red trails in its wake.

His heart pounded in his chest, the flickering lights causing that familiar static of an oncoming panic attack. He forced it aside for the time being, needed to focus. Colton took a closer look at one of the corpses. There was no telling what had happened. He was no coroner but judging by the state of the bodies in the room, and what little remained of them, he didn't think a coroner would do much better determining the cause of death.

This didn't look like the work of the Cleaver, that's for sure. The man was all about gruesome kills and horrible dismemberment, but whatever had happened here made the scene he'd walked in on earlier look like something from a PG-13 movie. No, this was something else.

Something worse, if the third body was any indication.

He'd been so fixated on the two ruined human forms, he had somehow glanced over the other *humanoid* form. He thought of it as humanoid because he'd never seen anything quite like it and had no words to describe the thing.

It had the general shape of a man, but the frame was a lean, muscular one, at least seven feet tall if the creature was bipedal. Long, striated muscles were visible under the parchment thin, paper-white, pale flesh. The thing had sharp, razor-like nails that extended a good three inches past the fingertips, curved and serrated.

Though the other two bodies were horribly dismantled, it was crystal clear what had killed the creature. There was a hole dead center in the forehead. Either a very good, or a very lucky shot. But from who? One of the other corpses in the room? Colton couldn't work his mind through the possibilities. How could he when the existence of the thing he was looking at was impossible?

The flickering lights were certainly no help. He needed a flashlight. Colton patted himself down but came away empty-handed. He'd forgotten his mini flashlight, a rookie mistake. He'd made a few mistakes on this mission that could have cost him more than the case. Perhaps it was time for him to hand in his resignation papers. The job wore the best Marshals down eventually, and Colton had buried himself in his work for so long that he was becoming a dried-out husk of a man.

But those were thoughts for another time. He had to see this through before he entertained such intrusive thoughts. His life, and many others, were on the line.

Colton flipped over the man he'd killed and searched him for anything that could be of use. He took the stun gun, the man's firearm, the master key card, and a flashlight. Tucked the items away best he could and scanned the room. In the back, there was a large panel smeared with blood. It was flanked on either side by two humongous cylinders. They looked like something out of a science fiction movie.

Both the large tubes were open, stinking of blood and rot.

"What the fuck is going on here?" Colton said to himself.

A terrifying, blood-curdling screech came from somewhere to his left, followed by a woman screaming. Colton pivoted in the direction the noise had come from, aiming the flashlight straight ahead.

A massive hole had been concealed by the darkness; the metal wall ripped open by something, possibly another one of those things.

Colton ran to the opening and, though he was no believer, made the sign of the cross before stepping through the sharp, jagged hole in the wall.

CHAPTER 20

Every footfall sent shocks of pain throughout Emily's entire body. Her heart raced a million miles an hour and the blood...the blood never stopped flowing. She wondered how long it would be until she lost too much and eventually pass out or die. Frantically pounding on every door she came across, despair settled in as no one dared to let in the bleeding, naked woman.

"Come on, open up!" she screamed at the last door in the sleeper car she was in. Nobody had answered her cries for help or her relentless pounding at the doors. She had no idea what time it was, and really, would it matter? She needed her husband and a way off the train. Who gave a shit what time it was?

She leaned her head against the door and pounded with both her fists. "Help me. Can you let me in?"

A door clicked, but it wasn't the one she was leaning on. Two doors down, a man stepped out of the cabin. Not just any man. It was the large bald man from earlier. He looked at her and smiled. "Emily, what a surprise! What happened to you?"

"William, I need help, please!" she said, stumbling toward him. She'd all but forgotten about the bad vibes he exuded earlier. Roxy was the real devil here. Her distrust of men had clouded her judgement. She noticed a large splash of blood covering his chest, and William looked down, noticing her gaze.

"Got into a fight with a gentleman at the bar," he said, taking a few steps toward her. He wrapped his arms around her, and she noticed he stunk of sweat and blood.

"Come now, I'll take care of you," he said. Emily was confused, but she was shaken, hurt, and needed help. She didn't know what else to do if William wasn't to be trusted. There was nobody else around. Against her better judgement, she allowed herself to be whisked away into the room he'd emerged from.

When they were last together, Emily had gotten a terrible feeling about this man. Now locked in his cabin, she realized she was correct, and she screamed in terror.

On the bed to their left lay a bloody husk of a woman. She was drenched in so much blood the sight reminded Emily of a dressed deer, its guts spilling out. William shoved her closer to the woman. She'd suffered far more than a deer would have.

"Come on, bitch. You denied me once. Now you get to watch before it's your turn."

William shoved her to the side of the room, and she fell over a small wooden chair with a red velvet cushion and arm rests. She was weak from loss of blood, and rather than attempt to flee, she cowered in the corner, praying for death. If there was a god, any god, it would be delivered swiftly.

"Don't fucking move or I will gut you," William

commanded. She was tempted to test him. Maybe he'd finish her sooner.

William pulled the cleaver from the woman's thigh. "That's my girl. We've got company. I hope you don't mind a bit of a show before you die."

Emily's stomach turned at the gruesome sight. The woman's chest had been sliced open down the middle and her flesh peeled back on either side, exposing muscle and bone underneath.

William looked back at Emily and ran a hand through the woman's bloody cavity, then stroked his now exposed cock with the bloody lube. He raised the cleaver over the woman's body with his left hand while still stroking himself with the other, then brought it down with a powerful force until it stuck in the woman with a meaty thud. William pulled the blade free and followed with another blow. William continued to stroke himself, alternating his gaze from the bloody woman in front of him and Emily, who'd suddenly decided she didn't want to die. What she'd witnessed was too gruesome. She'd rather take her chances with Roxy than this bastard, but she was powerless to escape. Maybe she'd die of blood loss before he turned his attention to her.

William grunted as if he were close to orgasm, but he clutched his cock tight, squeezing the head. He stayed there with his cock in a death grip for a few moments, still watching Emily, making sure she didn't move.

"Fuck yeah," he said. "Almost couldn't control myself there." He took a couple deep breaths and then looked at Emily.

"I don't know what the hell happened to you, but I'm

thankful you're back. Want a souvenir before you die?" He held up the woman's severed hand, the fingernails painted a bright pink. Blood dripped from near the wrist where it was attached moments before, one of Williams' strikes having severed it.

At last, Emily tried to run, but William had been ready for her to attempt to flee. He swatted her back down, easily.

"You know what…" William said, holding the hand and smiling at it. "I've got an idea. You're gonna love this."

William took the woman's dismembered hand and curled it around his cock, holding it in place with his own. "Yeah, that's it," he said. Then he proceeded to jack off with the woman's hand wrapped around his engorged member.

Emily's stomach twisted in disgust.

Like before, William pushed himself to the edge of orgasm before squeezing tight with the woman's hand. When he'd passed the point where the looming orgasm faded, he let go and tossed the woman's severed hand onto the bed. Emily gasped, the first sound she'd made since being dragged into this new nightmare.

"Like that, huh?" he said. "Sit back, sweetie. Your turn is next."

William grasped his blade and, with both hands, hacked into the bloody woman on the bed, not caring the woman was long dead and mutilated beyond recognition. He was distracted, Emily knew she'd get one more shot, and if she failed, she was dead.

Blood splashed onto William's bare chest and the man laughed maniacally. An arm came free, and he lifted it up like the Olympic torch, a symbol of his handiwork. He tossed it to the floor and continued to brutalize the woman with a smile permanently etched on his face.

A few blows later and he muttered, "Finally." William set the weapon down and reached inside the woman's body with both hands. He pulled out a long, bloody tube with ridges along the side.

Emily puked at the sight of the woman's intestines.

He wrapped the intestine around his cock. "Ribbed for my pleasure," he said, laughing at his own joke. William began to fuck the coiled intestine. He kept going, fucking the organ harder, grasping hold of them with both hands and thrusting like a madman. Emily tried hard not to vomit again. She needed to preserve as much of her energy as possible to get the fuck out of there, and she knew the time to strike was drawing near.

William groaned, a sound she'd heard from Kurt many times when he was about to blow his load. With as close as William had brought himself to orgasm earlier, there was no doubt it wouldn't take long for him to go.

"Fuck, yes!" he yelled. "Fuck, fuck!" He closed his eyes and yelled out as a thick stream of cum blasted from his cock and splashed inside the bloody cavity of the dead woman.

This is it. Now or never, Emily thought. Mustering the reserves of her strength, Emily jumped from her position on the floor and shoved William. Dizzy from his orgasm, he fell into the dead woman. Emily raced to the door.

"Get back here, you cunt!" William yelled. He'd gotten up from the woman, but Emily was committed to escaping. No matter what, she was going to get out. She grabbed the handle and spilled out into the hallway and then raced toward the far end of the car. Reaching the door that led to the next one over, she glanced back at William, who had tumbled out of the cabin and glared at her. Then, like an angry bull, he rushed at her. She fled through the door and plunged into the next car, hoping she had a chance to live.

This had been the train ride from hell, and she wanted nothing more than to take it back. They never should have punched their ticket to board the Coastal Express.

CHAPTER 21

S tepping through the hole, Colton walked into another horror show. The scene was much the same, entrails and viscera tossed about like a toddler playing with spaghetti. Multiple bodies in varying states of dismemberment. These kills appeared fresher. The door to this area, which seemed to be a storage area, lay in the hallway, battered off the frame. What the hell was going on here?

Sleepers. Colton remembered the word coming up in the investigation leading up to the mission multiple times. Did this current nightmare have something to do with whatever the fuck a sleeper was? Was that thing a sleeper? The thought spurred within his mind a quick brainstorm, images flashing in and out of existence in his mind, until he settled on something recent.

The large cylinders in the other room, and the odd equipment, panels, and wires connected to them.

"Jesus Christ," he muttered. He still wasn't completely sure what the hell was going on, but he was starting to make connections. And whether they were correct or not didn't change the fact that in addition to the Rail Car Cleaver running loose aboard the train, there were about a half dozen mutilated bodies between the room he stood in and the one he'd come from. There was some sort of mutant abomination lying dead in the other room, and if the appearance of two large tanks in the other room and the state of the one he stood in were any indicator, there was at least one more on the loose.

And that was assuming the two tanks in the other room were the only two tanks on the train.

Colton took off as fast as his feet would carry him, hopping over the battered door and into the hallway. He heard screams down the hall and sprinted toward the call to action.

Shouldering open the door to the next car, Colton immediately saw he had been correct. Another one of those things was loose, ripping and tearing at passengers.

The dining car was a mess. Bodies were everywhere. Some were still alive, most dead. Eviscerations, decapitations, amputations. The thing had done a number on quite a few people in a short amount of time.

The people who weren't yet injured or dead were trying to push their way through the crowd in a rush to escape, trampling over the fallen rather than helping them. The thing was perched on one of the dining tables, its head buried in a man's neck.

On the floor a few feet away, one man's corpse lay with its head crushed like a grape, a volcanic like eruption from the top of his head painting the carpets with a gruesome spray of skull fragment and brain matter.

Screaming, swearing, pushing, shoving. A woman fighting

through the crowd used her steak knife to slash at people in front of her, forcing her way through the crowd.

Colton pulled his pistol and aimed it at the creature, but he didn't have a clear line of sight. The bodies in the crowd kept getting in the way. If he were to take a shot at this range with a swarm of bodies, he had a better chance of hitting a passenger than that thing.

Behind him from the hallway he'd come through, a woman screamed.

More?

He turned around with his pistol ready to go but kept his finger off the trigger.

A naked woman was being chased by a naked bald man. The Coastal Express truly was something else.

It was the man he'd suspected to be the Rail Car Cleaver! Despite his nudity, he was gaining on the woman. Gone was the calm, cool demeanor from their earlier meeting. In its place was an unbridled rage. The man raised something over his head, the light catching the metal object just right, the gleam blinding Colton.

"Duck," Colton yelled at her.

She stumbled forward, hitting the ground. The woman had tripped, rather than ducking, but the fall saved her life just the same. She rolled underneath a table before recovering and disappearing into the writhing mass of bodies trying to escape the dining area.

The metal object flipped through the air over her head and struck Colton in the shoulder.

"Agghhh," he screamed, falling to the ground with a meat cleaver lodged between his left shoulder and pectoral muscle.

He hadn't considered the object might strike him when he told the woman to duck.

"You meddling little fuck," the man yelled. "If I hadn't told you pricks I'd be here on this train, you'd have never found me. You don't get to intervene. You and I don't settle this until *I'm* ready to put the finishing touches on this thing. But you've gone and fucked it up, haven't you?"

Colton heard the man, registered what he said, but the pain from the blade was making it difficult to concentrate.

William stood over Colton and ripped the blade from his body, blood spurting from the wound. He had no modesty, didn't seem to notice his bloody cock was dangling just over Colton's face while he prepared to butcher his next victims.

In the throng of people which had cleared out considerably, the creature screeched, the scent of fresh blood grabbing its attention from the corpse it was feasting upon.

"What the fuck is that?" William said.

It ran on all fours, lightning quick. Its claws shredding the carpet with each step, clicking against the flooring beneath the material.

The creature's terrifying vocalizations brought Colton back to reality, and he rolled under the nearest table.

A man attempting to escape the horror bumped into William. William grabbed him by the collar of his jacket, shoving him into the beast.

It leapt, crashing into the terrified man, pinning him to the ground. Its talons ripping and rending, blood and viscera spraying like a fountain.

Colton reached for the gun he'd dropped and aimed at the beast, but it must have heard him because it leapt off the man and onto the table he'd been underneath. He fired two shots up through the bottom of the table, neither of them hitting their mark.

The creature leapt off the table and tore a hole through the side of the car, exposing the cool night air. Trees and landscape raced by.

Colton watched it climb out of the car. It appeared to crawl up to the roof of the train, leaving nothing to look at but a blur of trees as they sped along the tracks.

The man Colton thought of as The Rail Car Cleaver extended a hand to Colton. "Truce?"

"The fuck I will," Colton said, slapping the hand away. There were creatures he couldn't explain, but he'd be damned if he'd work with a murderer. The man was covered in blood, no doubt from his latest victim.

"I don't see that you've got much of a choice, do you?" William said.

Colton seethed inside. He was there to apprehend this bastard, not work hand in hand with him.

"Why would you want to help?" Colton spat.

"Because I've got a feeling nobody is leaving this train alive if we don't get rid of that thing, and I want to get the fuck out of here."

"I don't trust you," Colton said. He couldn't believe he was entertaining the idea. Surely, he couldn't trust the man. He'd just tried to kill him!

"And I don't give a fuck who you trust. You have a gun and we've got a problem."

Colton grumbled. The piece of shit was right, and as much as he would hate to give the satisfaction, what other choice did Colton have?

"If we kill that thing, I'm taking you down," Colton said,

tearing his sleeve and using it to make a pressure dressing where the blade had bitten into his flesh.

William looked at Colton's shoulder. "I don't know that you're gonna last that long."

"If you want to get rid of that thing, you'd better hope I make it, because there was at least one more. The other one is dead, but until we find someone on this train who knows what the fuck is going on, we have to assume there could be more."

William looked at Colton with disgust. Saying nothing, he walked to one end of the car before returning with a white box with a red cross printed along the front. He tossed the first aid kit to Colton. "I'm going to enjoy killing you when this is over."

We'll see about that, Colton thought. "Just put some fucking pants on so we can get to work." Colton rummaged through the kit. Finding what he needed, he began to stitch the wound, wincing as he worked and finished the makeshift surgical work on his wounded shoulder.

CHAPTER 22

Emily thrust herself away from the monstrous creature that was ripping into another person in the dining car. *Holy fuck!* she screamed in her head. Had everyone turned into fucking psychos? Roxy. The bald man. Now there were some kind of nightmare creatures. Could that be what Roxy was talking about?

People were yelling and scrambling to get away from the horrible thing. Her worst nightmares didn't hold a candle to what she'd just stumbled into. The entire car was chaos. Gunshots went off. The man that had been chasing her lost track of her and instead had attacked another man. Emily shoved her way toward the exit. It was her only chance to escape this hell.

Emily snatched a clean dining napkin from one of the tables. She knew it would hurt, but she had no choice. She stuffed the cloth into her bleeding wound. It wouldn't stop the bleeding, but maybe it would slow it down long enough for her to escape.

Emily fled into the next car, which looked like an extension of the brutality she had just escaped. Battered and butchered bodies lay all over the hallway. The rich wooden walls were sprayed with blood and gore. Bone fragments and soft tissue clung like lichen on the wood. The stench of death was everywhere.

One of the cabin doors was open, the top half of a man's torso wedged between the door and the doorframe. Bloody entrails spilled out of his midsection like crimson snakes. When she peered inside, she noticed a stack of clean clothes and despite the urgent need to get the hell out of there, she was also completely nude and felt too exposed to continue. She stepped over the half man into the cabin. The other half of the man's body was on the floor in front of the couch, each leg bent at odd angles, his feet twisted around. Bones protruded through his bare flesh and his wounds wept blood. Emily fought back the urge to scream and snatched the clothes off the cabinet. They were the same train issued pants and shirt as she had on earlier. She slipped into them, and though it shouldn't have mattered in a life-or-death situation, covering her nude body made her feel more comfortable, somehow.

Emily closed her eyes and tried a calming exercise her therapist taught her after she'd discovered Kurt cheating. The therapist at the time hoped that by controlling her emotions, she'd gain clarity about the moment and see past her anger. It often worked. If there was ever a time to overcome her emotions, now was certainly it. If she couldn't keep herself in check, there was no way she would survive, and somewhere during the debacle with that psychopath she'd pushed aside the idea of wanting to die, instead choosing life. A few deep breaths later and she was about as calm as she was going to get, all things considered.

Back into the hallway it was a human slaughterhouse. Bloody body parts and desiccated bodies were everywhere. Some of the faces of the dead she recognized as people she'd seen at the bar or in the dining room. Others were staff members. Death seemed to know no bounds here.

It must be that creature, she thought. No way that sick, bald son of a bitch was responsible for all this carnage.

Emily stepped into the blood-soaked hall and turned to the right, toward the other exit leading to the next train car. There was no fucking way she was going back to the dining car with the bald man, the guy with the gun, and that thing. Let them deal with it.

She carefully walked through the gore, trying her damnedest not to step onto bits of muscle and flesh. She was still barefoot and wanted to avoid squishing her toes into something that once was housed inside of a person.

Near the end of the hall, she stepped into a thick puddle of warm blood and felt something soft under her foot. It was fleshy and pliant. She held back the vomit trying to escape her mouth, grabbed the door handle, and moved to the next car.

Unlike the previous one, this car was almost entirely devoid of any sign of the massacre she had just escaped. Instead, it held a more sterile feeling and was significantly colder than the previous car. A soft hum like some sort of equipment was running droned on.

Instead of normal doors lining the right side of the car, there were three handles that reminded her of large walk-in freezers. She crept toward the closest one and tried the handle. It creaked open.

True to her first impressions, it was a cooler, but it took her a moment to realize what she was looking at.

The yellow overhead light inside flickered, and she stood frozen in place.

Metal wire shelves lined each side. Thin strips of meat were stacked in pans on one side of the cooler. Deep red, it looked like beef. But then, across from that on the other rack, three heads were looking back at her, their eyes open and their faces gaunt as though they'd been drained. What the hell was going on here?

One of the heads was Kurt.

"Oh fuck! No, no, no, no!" she cried. Emily took a step closer, not believing that what she was looking at was her husband. It couldn't be. It was impossible. Why the hell would his head be on a rack inside a cooler?

The longer she looked at it, the more the reality set in. This *was* Kurt. The bastards from the train had taken him away after he got sick, and they must have done this to him. A powerful surge of grief welled up inside her.

"No!" she screamed, tears streaming down her face. When had they done this to him? Was he still alive when she had cheated on him with Roxy?

She grabbed his head and peered into his lifeless eyes.

"I'm so fucking sorry," she muttered through her tears. "I'm so sorry." Grief chased away the fear she'd been running from moments ago. Nothing mattered anymore. Kurt was dead. Most of the passengers were dead.

And yet the train continued to rumble down the tracks.

Emily slunk down in the cooler until she was seated on the cold metal floor. She rested Kurt's head on her lap and cradled it with both hands so that they were looking at one another. Tears continued to run down her cheeks.

Despite their problems, despite the infidelity, this was her husband. Kurt was her everything. Now, he was relegated to a blood-drained head resting in her grasp.

She closed her eyes and cried, letting the madness of the situation consume her.

Within her grief, she was vaguely aware of the cooler door creaking open. She gasped. So stupid of her to not shut the door.

That thing from earlier had found her.

Emily's eyes went wide. Her heart raced, panic pushing aside her grief. The thing peered at her, blood dripping from its lips and coating its chest. It licked its lips and opened its mouth filled with sharp, jagged teeth. She glanced down at Kurt's head, then back at the creature. After all she'd been through, dying might not be the worst thing.

Colton watched the Cleaver strip a corpse of its trousers and don the man's pants. If he didn't know the man to be the most notorious active serial killer, he'd have laughed at the sight of the man wearing tattered, high-water trousers. Still, he couldn't help smirking. Something about the pants hardly reaching the psychopath's ankle struck Colton's funny bone.

William noticed Colton smiling. "Something funny, Marshal? Have you ever heard of privacy? Can a man put his pants on without the prying eyes of the law? You know, I almost never figured you out. If you hadn't seen me with that woman, I might never have guessed who you were."

"And I wasn't even at the top of my game. You're nothing. You did what you did here because I fucked up, but I'm not gonna be taking my eyes off you until you're locked in a cage like the animal you are."

"Wonderful. I hope you know I'll never be taken in by you. I can see it in your eyes. You're tired. You don't have the killer instinct in you anymore. You might be determined to do your job, but you don't have the nuts to do what needs to be done." He grabbed his crotch as if to emphasize his point.

Colton wondered if it was true. Sure, he'd gone toe to toe with some bad dudes on the train, but there were dead bodies everywhere, and Colton still hadn't taken his man down, nor had he put a stop to whatever the fuck was going on aboard the train. Had he gotten soft? More thoughts to table for future retrospective. For now, he needed to work with the slimeball known as The Rail Car Cleaver and save the rest of the people on the train. If there was ever a time to have a notorious serial killer on your side, now was the time.

The crowd of people had mostly dispersed, but a handful of the riders were still in the room in various states of mental and physical debilitation. A woman cowered in the corner, strips of flesh hanging from her face, blood puddling around her. She sat, waiting to die. A man lay on the floor in the fetal position, babbling hysterically. Body parts and viscera were tossed haphazardly across the room, blood dripping from the ceiling, from the walls, from the tables. Colton had never seen anything like it before.

"We should go talk to the conductor. He would know what's going on," Colton suggested.

"Sure. But how about you give me a gun so I can defend myself?"

"I'm not giving you a damn gun. Why don't you use your cleaver? You seem to be an expert with it."

"Mmm, you're right about that. Still, I'd like to put some distance between myself and that thing if it comes back to finish what it started."

"Well, you're shit out of luck, because I'm not giving you a gun. You find one on a body, fine, but the moment I see you so much as look sideways at myself, or one of the passengers, I'm going to put a hole in the center of your fucking head."

"Noted. Why don't we get to the bottom of this and then you can take your best shot?"

"You first buddy, I'm not letting you out of my sight."

Colton followed The Cleaver, giving the man directions as they followed the signs to the front of the train. He tried his best to drown out the noise, but the screams and cries seemed to come from everywhere. Had the beast found more victims? Or were these coming from the passengers whose lives had been turned upside down by a nightmare creature?

Blood squelched under Colton's shoes and a loud crack of thunder seemed to split the sky itself. Colton didn't jump, didn't so much as twitch. He was finally tuned in, the well-oiled machine reactivated, at least for the time being. Maybe the lunatic had been right, maybe he *had* lost the spark he once had for the job. But, if he *had* lost that spark, that killer instinct, then the atrocity he'd just witnessed had stoked the flames once more.

CHAPTER 24

A loud boom from above pulled the creature's attention from the sounds of the train below it. Preternatural senses, a mixture of its mother's abilities, and those spliced into it through human meddling, allowed it to hunt its prey in the worst of conditions, but its highly attuned senses could be a hindrance, especially when it had yet to acclimate to its surroundings.

A heavy downfall of precipitation pelted the monstrosity's skin as the rain's petrichor scent assaulted the thing's olfactory organs.

But the need to hunt, the need for blood and flesh, imparted upon it from its mother, was too strong for anything to grab its attention for long. It was voracious. Its thirst, unquenchable. Its hunger, uncontrollable.

There was one thing that matched its impulse to feed—the instinct to protect its kin. One of the prey had managed to destroy its brother, and it had made the thing pay dearly. It sensed two more of its kin, a gentle tug below the surface of its consciousness. They, too, were awake. The moment their brother's life had been extinguished, it felt them rise from their slumber.

And Mother. Mother was in pain. Immense pain. Her screams pierced the back of its mind, overwhelming the creature.

The animals below would come later. It would feed after dealing with Mother's screams.

The creature had no sense of time. It ran on instinct alone. Just a few short minutes had passed since it abandoned the hunt, instead turning its attention toward its dying mother. Atop the train, it stopped over one of the cars, tilted its head to the sky and screeched at the clouds. Thunder clapped, drowning its howls. Countryside flew by, trees and dirt roads a blur as the monstrosity tore its way through the roof of the train car, dropping into the room below.

Roxy sat on the floor, sucking blood from her mangled arm. More of the crimson fluid came out of her midsection in a steady stream. She was pale, gaunt. The scent of blood had been too much for her to resist and so she fed on herself. She looked up at her progeny.

"How did you escape? They told me there was no way," she said, her voice a cracked, withered thing.

The creature didn't understand the vocalizations of its mother, but it sensed her pain and fear.

"I can't believe I let them use my bloodline to create something like you. No money is worth this. They say my kind are monsters, but you are something else," she said, trying to scramble backward, but unable to move, far too weak from her wounds.

Mother was stronger than the animals that looked like her, but not as strong as her progeny. "Get away from me!" she screamed.

The creature hissed at Roxy, confused by the fear and anger it sensed coming off her in waves. It couldn't understand what Roxy was saying, but it understood her body language and sensed *it* was the reason for mother's fear and anger. Why? It had done her no harm.

With her good arm, Roxy grabbed a drinking glass from the counter and flung it at the creature, striking it in the head. The throw was weak, but the glass still shattered. Green blood oozed from the cut along where the hairline would be if the creature weren't hairless.

The creature roared in anger. Embattled with its mother's hatred, and now her assault, it lashed out. The thing leapt the few feet of distance between itself and its mother, claws outstretched, ready to rip and tear.

It landed on Roxy's back as she attempted to turn and get up, pinning her to the ground. Her screams of pain, once a beacon to the monstrosity, now served to increase the animalistic pleasure it took from the hunt. The creature tore at her back, flaying flesh, sending ribbons of it in every direction and painting the room in gore.

The creature dug its way through flesh and muscle, lapping at blood and swallowing meat.

At some point, Roxy stopped screaming, but the creature never noticed. Its voracious appetite had long overshadowed her cries of pain and terror.

Chapter 25

"Do you see that?" Emily heard a voice from beyond the cooler door, behind the creature.

"I think we're almost there," another voice replied. She couldn't be sure, but they sounded familiar. The sound of other people gave her hope. Maybe they'd help her. Or maybe they'd distract the creature long enough for her to escape.

The creature stepped closer, sniffing the cool air and licking its lips. Emily had no weapon and no way of defending herself. Glancing down at her husband's head, an idea struck her, though it wasn't one she was proud of. She couldn't save Kurt, but maybe he could still save her. *I'm so sorry*, she thought.

Slowly rising to her feet, she clutched Kurt's head with one hand while the creature inched forward. She saw its muscles tense and knew her plan had to work or she would die.

The creature lunged at her, snapping its jaws.

Emily jumped back and slammed into the cooler wall. She held Kurt's severed head in front of her like a shield and shoved it into the creature's open mouth. Shocked by the object stuck in its jaws, the thing screeched, clutching at the head. Emily bolted past the thing while it was distracted. She reached the cooler door and pushed on the handle. Behind her, a sickening crunch forced her to look back. The thing had crushed into Kurt's skull with the force of its bite. Bits of bone and shards of teeth sprinkled to the floor. Emily's stomach twisted into a knot, but she couldn't dwell on it for long. If she didn't escape, the thing would do the same to her.

Emily pushed through the door and slammed it closed behind her, leaving the beast to finish dining on Kurt's head. Her wound ached and throbbed but she had no time to deal with it now.

She sobbed, her back to the door as two men approached her.

"Hey, are you ok?" one of them asked. His voice was authoritative and familiar. She turned and her eyes bulged. It was the man who'd tried to shoot the psychopath earlier. But he was *with* that fucker. Were they working together? Why would he have warned her to duck if that were so?

"Hey, I'm here to help," the man said, hands still ready on his gun. She took a step back, her eyes fixated on the bald man.

"Come on, bitch, I wasn't done with you," the bigger man said.

The man with the gun spoke again. "You remember what I told you before? I don't mind putting a bullet in you here and now."

A thump against the cooler door sent her leaping across the aisle. Both men turned in the direction of the sound.

"Come on, we're getting the hell out of here. Either that

thing is back, or it's another one entirely. Who knows how many there are," the man with the gun said.

He seemed to have an authority about him, and at least for the time being, the lunatic bald son of a bitch seemed to do what the man with the gun told him. Was he a cop? Or was he in charge by default because he had a gun?

As if he'd read her mind, he spoke. "I'm Robert Colton. I'm a U.S. Marshal. You can trust me."

"I don't trust him," she said. Then as an afterthought, she added, "I'm Emily."

A louder thump from inside and then a noise like metal tearing.

"I don't trust him either, but we've got to go now." Colton said.

"Ok," she said, falling in line next to the Marshal, but keeping away from the psychopath.

"Don't even fucking think about harming her. Got it?" Colton said.

"Yeah, yeah. You said that already."

Colton looked at her. "Emily," he said, "I mean it. We need him, but I'll kill him if he tries anything. Now let's go. We're out of time." She nodded. This uncomfortable alliance was one of necessity, not choice.

The beating on the cooler door behind her grew more intense and the metallic shrieking grew louder, the layers of the door peeling away. A bang and the handle moved down. Had it figured out how to use a door handle? Again, the handle moved farther.

Once more, and the handle dropped all the way, the door inching open. The creature leapt from inside and turned in their direction. It snarled and raced toward them.

"Oh fuck!" William yelled. Emily felt heavy hands on her back that pushed her toward the thing. She landed on her face, the wind escaping her lungs. The creature was only a few feet away from her.

Colton yelled, but Emily didn't know what he was saying, her own pulse loud in her ears. Gunshots fired and Emily's ears rang from the shots. The aim was true, and the bullets punctured the creature's chest. It reared back, screaming.

Colton was at her side and wrapped an arm around her, pulling her to her feet and shoving her behind him. She stumbled but caught herself. The door from the train car to the next clicked, and she glanced back to see William escaping into the next one over. Colton grumbled.

The creature howled, thrashing in the hall. Green blood had splashed on the walls and the floor, the bullet wounds bleeding profusely, though the thing was still very much alive.

"Stay behind me," Colton commanded. The creature lunged, and Colton fired three more shots. The first shot, and then another, struck its arm. The third punched through its eyeball. A spray of green blood erupted from the bullet's exit at the back of its skull. Its head whipped back, and it fell to the floor. Blood oozed from the wounds. It took a deep breath and then its chest stopped moving.

"Son of a bitch!" Colton yelled. "I swear to God I'm going to kill that motherfucker. Are you ok?" he asked.

"Once I find out there are no more of those things, I've got a bullet for him. Come on, we have one more car and then I think we'll get to the engine. We have to stop this train and get the fuck off."

Emily nodded. She was numb and at this point just going

along with the man who claimed to be a law enforcement. It didn't seem she had much else of a choice.

CHAPTER 26

William led the way, followed by Colton and Emily. He'd been waiting in the next car after muscling Emily to the floor. Coward. No way Colton was turning his back to that lunatic, and he sure as shit wasn't going to allow William to be out of sight with Emily. He had half a mind to put a bullet in the man right now and end it, but he might need him to take care of those things, if there were more.

At first, Colton wasn't sure about Emily. She'd been a mess when they found her, but give credit where credit is due - she stopped crying, set her grief aside, and chose to survive, rather than shut down and die.

Most of the crowd had dispersed, either brutally dispatched by one of those things, or hiding in their rooms. But they weren't safe. Colton knew that. He had watched one of those fuckers rip its way out of the side of the train, tearing the locomotive like it was nothing more than a sheet of paper.

Advancing their way through the car, none of them spoke. William had tried to break the silence, but Colton shut it down, and Emily ignored him. He hadn't said anything since.

Colton's heart jackhammered against his ribs, and he felt weak. Before using the first aid kit, he'd lost a good amount of blood. It hadn't been enough to kill him at the moment, but the waves of dizziness could very well cost him his life in a battle with those things, or even against William. The firearm gave him the upper hand, but he only had so many bullets left, and no idea how many of those things were lurking.

At the end of the corridor, William stopped. "We're here," he said, pointing to the sign mounted next to a shut door.

"Open it up," Colton said.

William tried the handle. "It's locked."

"Try again," Colton said. He'd just watched William *pretend* to open the door. The man was obviously trying to get Colton to turn his back to him. Whether it was to take an opportunity at Colton, or at Emily, he wasn't sure. Either way, he wasn't going to fall for it.

William sighed, then slid the door open.

They entered the front of the train. The engineer sat with his back to them, operating the train as if he were oblivious to everything that had transpired.

"You've gotta stop the train," Colton shouted.

The engineer ignored him, keeping his eyes forward, enveloped in the task of operating the train. Through the glass windshield, Colton could see rain coming down heavy and hard, masking the way forward.

William grabbed the man's shoulder and barked, "Stop the fucking train or you die!"

Colton raised his pistol, pointing at William. "Nobody else dies," he said.

A shriek from behind them and the sound of crumpling steel as one of the creatures smashed the door down. Emily jumped back, narrowly avoiding the door, bumping into Colton.

The creature slashed, swiping at Emily. Its claws lacerated her flesh, and she screamed in response.

Colton shoved her aside, harder than he meant to, but he couldn't think about her now. He had to take this thing down. He aimed at the creature and fired two rounds, but the thing had already leapt to the side before he'd pulled the trigger. Its speed was uncanny. Colton had no doubt whoever had put a bullet between the eyes of the one he'd seen dead earlier had simply gotten a lucky shot. He was a good shot, but watching these things in action left no doubt his own bullseye had been luck more than skill. There were no bullet wounds on this one, so it couldn't be the one from the dining car, which meant this was yet *another* of those things. Either that or they could heal so long as they weren't dead. Colton wasn't sure which option was worse.

The creature stood on its rear legs, screeching, puffing its body up as large as it could go in a show of force. Colton fired, the ringing in his ears from shooting indoors dulling the reports of gunfire within the engineer's cabin.

The creature leapt again, dodging another bullet and taking a chance at William, who stepped to the side and swung his blade.

He wasn't quick enough to avoid the blow, and the creature's razor claws split his flesh like an over-ripe fruit.

The blade fell to the ground, and William's arm fell alongside it as the last strand of flesh tore away, leaving a stump at the elbow.

William screamed and dropped to the floor.

The creature turned its attention to the engineer, who'd

stopped watching the train's progress to stare at the horror show happening in his cabin.

Colton ignored William's cries for help. Instead, he raised the pistol at the creature that now had its face buried in the crook of the engineer's neck. He fired the pistol until it clicked empty. Blood spurted from the wounds, but the thing paid no mind, finishing its meal.

Colton dug through his pockets for a spare clip, but it was gone, along with the pistol he'd swiped from a body earlier. He must have dropped them in his haste.

"Fuck," he shouted. He really had lost his edge. Weapon retention was basic. Law enforcement 101. He'd slipped up and it might cost him his life.

On the floor, William managed to stop panicking and fight through the pain. He used the belt of his pants as a tourniquet. The man looked like shit, covered in blood, and he'd turned pale white.

The creature tossed the engineer aside, leaving him slumped against the controls where the deadweight of his body forced the train to accelerate.

Colton helped Emily to her feet, and William managed to stand upright. They all had the same idea—get the fuck out of dodge. They ran, Colton helping Emily along as William hobbled after them. The blood from his severed wound slowed to a trickle now.

The creature stalked slowly behind them. It seemed to have determined they were no longer a threat, and it was merely a predator toying with its prey.

The train, now traveling at top speed, whisked along the track, cutting through the onslaught of rain as it approached the curve with nobody to slow it down.

Colton felt a shift below his feet as the train took the curve, too fast, along the soaked tracks. First, there was a loud, metallic crash, followed by violent jostling as the train's wheels left the tracks and the large transport vehicle listed to the side, teetering before finally flipping over.

The metal vehicle shrieked and banged as the train flipped, the impact crumpling the train and shredding it in places.

Colton flew through the air. The last thing he saw before the impact knocked him unconscious was the ceiling of the train rapidly approaching as he fell downward toward it.

CHAPTER 27

William lowered himself to the ceiling, which was now located underneath him. Despite all odds, he had somehow survived. The moment he'd felt the train lurch, he dove underneath a table, and while he wouldn't have thought that would have saved his bacon, the table being bolted to the floor of the train had allowed him to hang on for dear life.

From what William had seen, Colton hadn't fared as well. The man may still have all his limbs, but he'd been ping-ponged around the train like a child's plaything. As for Emily, William didn't see what happened to her during the accident. Turns out a freshly severed appendage made it difficult to focus on your surroundings.

He took a deep breath and coughed. A thick, black smoke billowed through the train's interior. William smelled the fire, though he couldn't see it. It was time to disembark the Coastal Express. He'd had his fun with quite a few passengers this trip and managed to evade capture despite taunting the law enforcement agencies, going so far as telling them exactly where he'd be. So, what if he didn't kill the woman? He'd whetted his blade plenty. And if he made it through this, there would be plenty more to come.

A cool breeze entered the train through a shattered window off to William's side. The creature that had attacked them lay twitching. A large pole impaled it through the abdomen, pinning it to the floor. Green blood oozed around the dying creature.

William stooped down and picked up his cleaver, ready to finish the beast off and exit the train. Off to the side, he heard someone moan. "Oh, this just keeps getting better," he said.

COLTON'S HEAD felt like it was in a vise. His entire body screamed in pain. The train had derailed and somehow…he survived. Burning electric wires and diesel fuel mixed with smoke and dirt. He tried moving his legs, but they failed to respond. *Jesus Christ, I'm fucking crippled*, he thought. But he wasn't sure. His legs hurt, so maybe, despite the unimaginable pain, that was actually a good thing. Unable to move and sure death was soon to follow, he reflected on the mission. A lot of good he'd done by coming on this stupid fucking train. He hadn't saved anyone, and the Rail Car Cleaver was likely dead and would never be brought to justice. He deserved to rot in prison for his crimes before eventually dying a slow, agonizing death. Whatever happened to the man here wasn't punishment enough.

Colton closed his eyes. Would he finally see Jessica again? He hoped more than anything. He didn't need closure. Didn't need to know what happened to her. He now longed only to be reunited with his daughter.

He heard footsteps crunching the twisted metal and broken glass. Colton looked up and knew it was time.

EMILY'S EYES were locked on the bone jutting from her arm. The pain was immense, but the adrenaline flooding her body had kept the worst of it at bay during the accident, but now, the adrenaline was receding, replaced with a screaming pain.

Where were the others? Had Colton and the lunatic both survived? Hopefully Colton had. With any luck, that monster was lying dead somewhere. The world didn't need monsters like him.

Another shock of pain radiated out from her chest. Breathing grew difficult. Looking down, her situation became clear to her. Somehow a post that had once held up a dining table had punched through her body. Chunks of flesh and muscle hung from its jagged metal tip.

Blood bubbled in her mouth. The light was fading fast. Someone moved in the wreckage. Her vision fading fast, she couldn't tell who it was. She thought it was that lunatic. The man was large. At least she would die without giving him the satisfaction of ushering her into the next life.

WILLIAM MADE his way gingerly toward Colton. Every step made his body ache.

"You survived, huh," Colton muttered, "it's always the pieces of shit who seem to live." Colton coughed. Crimson tinged droplets of blood mixed with spittle flew from his mouth.

"I'm gonna enjoy this. I always do," William said, bringing the cleaver down, striking Colton's shoulder. The man screamed, and William laughed. He'd meant to hit Colton's neck, but he was weak and using his non-dominant hand. William chose to look on the bright side. He'd get to give the Marshal a few more chops for good luck.

William brought the cleaver down twice more, blood splattering his chest and face.

"See you in hell." He brought the blade down one last time, burying it in Colton's neck.

Tired, William pulled the cleaver from Colton's neck and let it hang at his side. A few pumps of blood squirted from the man's carotid artery before at last it stopped spurting and simply ran out.

Satisfied with his handiwork, William made his way past the still dying creature, easily avoiding the thing's weak attempts to swipe him as he crawled through the window.

Outside, he got to his feet, stumbled, and caught his balance. The cool rain felt good on his battered body. He had made it out alive and was still a free man. William would live to kill another day.

He surveyed his surroundings. The train had derailed and flipped on the country hillside, but in the distance, he saw the lights of a small town. Perfect. He would make his way there and call emergency services. Hospitals couldn't turn someone away. There would be nothing connecting him to the murders on the train. He could think of an excuse on the way. Maybe he'd escaped from some deranged men who'd held him captive and tortured him. He wouldn't be able to lead anyone to the fabricated house he'd talk about. It didn't exist. But who could blame him for not remembering how to get back with all the blood he'd lost? He could see it now. They'd chalk it up to a mental block, his psyche protecting him from the memory of what he'd endured.

William took a tentative step away from the tree he'd used for support and his head swam. Maybe he wasn't out of the woods yet. He might well die from loss of blood before making it to the village. Slowly, he began his trek toward the lights in the distance.

He shivered. The rain no longer felt good, and progress had been slow. He was weak, too weak. William leaned against another tree, taking a breather. His eyelids fluttered, heavy.

From the train came a screeching noise. His eyes shot open and the hair on his neck stood at attention. Two more screeches followed the first.

Spurred into action, William found the strength to soldier on. He marched toward the town, but no matter which direction he went, death was sure to follow.

Acknowledgments

Jay Bower

Thank you for riding the Coastal Express. We hope your trip was enjoyable.

I have to begin by thanking my co-author and friend John Lynch.

We met at AuthorCon2 in 2023 and have remained friends ever since. John and I had been talking about co-writing a novel even before we released *The Conservator's Collection: Derelict* (with John Durgin) and we both had the time in our busy schedules to make it work, so we went for it. We wanted to write a campy, bloody, gnarly story that was reminiscent of our love for late 80s and early 90s B-horror movies and I feel like we succeeded. We just had fun with it and I hope it came through in the story.

I'd like to thank early readers Stephanie Huddle and Dottie Sargent for their ~~sacrifice~~ critiques. Your insight was super valuable.

I'd like to thank Candace Nola for her edits and helping make our story better.

Our cover was from Matt Seff Barnes who does amazing work. If you need a cover, check him out!

All the authors that have encouraged me and helped me along the way: John Durgin, Megan Stockton, David Viergutz, Gage Greenwood, Duncan Ralston, Nick Roberts, Mike Evans, Andrew Van Wey, Bridgett Nelson, and so many others. The community of horror authors is a small, tight-knit group and I'm so thankful for sharing all of this with you.

My Patrons have been super encouraging and supportive. Thank you all for making the Cellar a special place. I'm so grateful to all of you. You rock!

For my readers in Bower's Basement of Humanity, thanks for hanging out with me under the stairs.

Finally, I want to give thanks to my family for supporting me and letting me pursue this passion of telling stories. I couldn't ask for more. I love you.

Dear reader, thanks again for your time. I'm unbelievably humbled by your continued support. Every new book I release is a nerve-wracking experience because I want to respect your time with my stories and I hate to disappoint you. I appreciate you and look forward to sharing more stories with you.

Stay scary,
  -Jay
  June 14, 2024

Patrons

Jay Bower

My Patrons are amazing. I cannot thank you all enough for what you've done for me. Your support means more than you will ever truly know. I want to give a special shout out to those that are at the *Wraith of Dreams* and higher tiers:

Dottie Sargent

Jason Artz

Lisa Breanne

Mary T.

Charlotte Stevenson

Deven V.

Stephanie Huddle

Tiqua L.

Candace N.

Megan S.

Molly Mix

Savannah Fischer

Steve S.

If you'd like to join Jay's Cellar Dwellers and get exclusive stories and early access to new material, please check out my Patreon at patreon.com/cellardwellers.

About the Author

Jay Bower

Jay Bower is a horror author living outside St. Louis, MO in the forest of Southern Illinois. He spends his time reading, writing, and convincing his wife the dark stories he writes do not involve her.

For links to all his books, visit his website. There you can also get a free story for signing up to his reader list.

jaybowerauthor.com

facebook.com/jaybowerauthor

x.com/JayBowerAuthor

instagram.com/jaybowerauthor

tiktok.com/@jaybowerauthor

Acknowledgments
John Lynch

First, thank you to my family for your support and encouragement. Instead of telling me I can't, you all tell me I can.

Thank you to my good friend, Jay Bower, for tackling this crazy story with me. After *Conservator's Collection*, Jay and I knew we wanted to work together again, this time on a collaborative book rather than an anthology. Jay has become a good friend of mine, and we talk daily. I'm thankful to have met him at Authorcon 2.

We were pitching ideas back and forth and after a few minutes came up with the idea of a hedonistic train where people get murdered. We both thought it would be fun to have a book that read like a sleazy, b-movie horror from the VHS days. Plenty of explicit sex and gore. But I didn't want to just do a slasher. I felt like much of my stuff, if technically not a slasher, shares many elements of them. And Christmas Eve Carnage, my previous release most definitely is a slasher. So we came up with this idea for an explicit slasher/creature feature. It would fit with the b-movie vhs vibe and would allow us to really embrace the craziness. In the end, we settled on the story you've just read. It is violent, gory, explicit, and most of all, doesn't take itself too seriously. We toyed around a bit about how much to explain, and what to explain, and in the end settled for what I think really is the difference between a b-movie that works, and one that doesn't. There have to be some questions. The more you explain things, the more you're leaving things open for people to rip apart. So yes, there is a seedy corporate duo that is uber rich. But we don't tell you too much about them. Yes, they are selling these creatures, bioweapons, to the highest bidders, including terrorist groups. But it isn't explicitly spelled out, It is alluded to in one bit of dialogue in the book. The creatures came from a vampire's bloodline, a scientific experiment done by the duo using Roxy's blood. The normal vampires in this world are strong enough, but they aren't like something you'd see in Blade, or 30 days of night. They feed on blood, they live a long time, they're a bit stronger and faster than humans. But as you can see, they aren't invincible, and someone like Emily can get the better of them. I do believe sometimes it is better to just take readers along for the ride, rather than hold their hands and explain everything. If that approach didn't work for you, I apologize. Don't hold that against Jay, I was the one who suggested we leave things as vague as possible.

Shout-out to the Palooza. You all know who you are. All the members of my Patreon.

Thanks to John Durgin, Brennan LaFaro, Gage Greenwood, Duncan Ralston, Matt Seff Barnes, Brian Berry, Judith Sonnet, David Viergutz, Mark Tulius, Candace Nola, Daniel J. Volpe, Kiera Dervisevic, and many more.

As usual, Aron Beauregard gets his own paragraph. I'm positive I annoy the shit out of him, so I try to ask as little as possible, but he has always helped me to grow and guided me in the right direction when I ask. Thank you, brother. I appreciate you. Thank you to all of the readers out there who continue to support me. I first published *The Warrior Retreat* in

November of 2022 and the support and enthusiasm everyone has show toward my books is truly something special. Whether you enjoyed my books, or not, I appreciate that you spent your money, and took the time to read my books. There are so many choices out there, so many authors and so many books, and from the bottom of my heart, I thank you for picking up my books.

JL 06/14/2024

Patrons

John Lynch

John would like to thank ALL the members of his patreon for helping to support his dream of writing for a living. The following members are subscribed to the Corporal tier or higher.

Tiqua L.

Sara F.

Gage G.

Charlotte S.

Andy

Mary T.

Kristina L.

Kayla

If you are interested in short stories, serialized books, non fiction essays, writing tips, conversational videos, you can check out his patreon here: patreon.com/johnlynchbooks

About the Author

John Lynch

John Lynch is a Horror writer and Marine Corps veteran from Rhode Island.

johnlynchbooks.com

X x.com/johnlynchbooks
instagram.com/johnlynchbooks
tiktok.com/@johnlynchhorror